Merlin

Strayed, But Not Lost

A novel. Vol. 1

Merlin

Strayed, But Not Lost
A novel. Vol. 1

ISBN/EAN: 9783337149567

Printed in Europe, USA, Canada, Australia, Japan

Cover: Foto ©Andreas Hilbeck / pixelio.de

More available books at **www.hansebooks.com**

STRAYED,
BUT NOT LOST.

A Novel in Two Volumes.

By MERLIN.

VOL. I.

LIVERPOOL:
ROWLAND A. ELLIOTT, 42 CANNING PLACE.
LONDON: E. W. ALLEN, STATIONERS' HALL COURT.

1876.

PREFACE.

An opinion appears to prevail that every woman who makes one false step, *must* have a natural tendency to vice, and that she is thenceforth utterly lost to all sense of shame. In the following pages the Author has endeavoured, in what he ventures to hope may be found a readable story, to contradict this theory, and to show that with fair opportunities, and kind, instead of harsh treatment, such a woman may prove not only a devoted wife and an excellent mother, but an ornament to her sex.

In the hope of dispersing that which he cannot but regard as altogether a fallacy, and inducing some of his readers to "temper justice with mercy," this work is confidently given to the Public by

THE AUTHOR.

CONTENTS.

STRAYED, BUT NOT LOST.

CHAPTER I.

MORS JANUA VITÆ.

"Hark, they whisper—angels say,
'Sister spirit, come away!'"

PORE.

"Is there any hope, Doctor?" asked a tall,
powerful-looking young man of one or two-
and-twenty years of age.

He spoke calmly, but the very calmness and
deliberation with which the words were pro-
nounced betrayed the fierce struggle for the
mastery between the feelings and the utterance of a strong man.

"Monsieur," replied the accoucheur, evasively, "the life of Madame is in the hands
of the good God."

"Yes, yes," impatiently rejoined the first
speaker, "but in your opinion as a medical
man, is there any chance of her recovery?"

"Madame is very, very ill," was the somewhat aggravating reply.

The young man turned savagely on the
tender-hearted little doctor, and seizing him
by the shoulders, shook him violently.

"Come, come," cried he; "prevarication is
as useless as it is unseemly—the truth—the
truth — I must bear it; there is then no
hope?"

The doctor's voice faltered as he laconically
answered, "none."

What is more touching, more heart-rending
to witness than the agony of a strong man?

The wretched husband essayed to speak,
but a choking sensation in his throat denied
him utterance, and after pressing the hand
of the kind little doctor he waved him away,

and gently opening the door of the chamber (outside which the above conversation had taken place) walked on tip-toe to the side of the bed on which lay his dying wife.

She had been married scarcely more than twelve months, and within the last few hours had given birth to a daughter. She appeared at least ten years older than her husband, but was in reality two or three years younger. A year ago she was fresh, gay and beautiful as any of nature's fairest flowers; and now, pale, careworn and prematurely aged, she lay on her death-bed. The hand of Death was upon her, it needed no practised eye to trace the prints of his cruel nails.

Reader! it is hard to die so young! life is very, very sweet. They who, in the prime of youth and strength, can welcome Death with out-stretched hand have never lived. How many have we known who for years have *existed*, but never lived! What is *Death* to them? 'Tis but the snapping of the thread of existence. How can such as these crave for those delicious draughts of life and pleasure which they have never tasted? But they who have lived and loved, who have drained to the very dregs the brimming cup of pleasure, who have lived not only for themselves but for another, who have been blessed with eyes to see and ears to hear, who have recognized and appreciated all and every of nature's beauties and wonders; can such, we ask, throw off this mortal coil without regret? Reader! be not fooled by hypocrites and religious enthusiasts! We tell you it *is* hard for such to die.

The husband's eyes filled with tears as he gazed on the features of the dying girl. For the first time he realized the awful fact that he was the cause of the wreck of the good ship, which he should have piloted in safety through the troubled waters of life. In an agony of grief he threw himself on his knees at the bed-side, and for the first time in his life prayed. His prayer was short, " My God, spare her ! "

Since her marriage the poor girl had lived

but for one object—his happiness; *he* was her centre, her all. And how had her thoughtless husband appreciated her devotion and love? He had neglected her. No harsh words, no cruel blows, had ever passed; no kinder or better intentioned husband ever lived; but he had been thoughtless and selfish, and night after night had he left her alone,—alone in Paris,—without friends, without any amusement, to watch the clock and count the weary hours which must pass before his return from the gambling-house, or from the house of some of his wild and dissipated acquaintances. To a woman of his wife's nature, this treatment meant death by slow torture.

The birth of her child was soon to cut short the thread of an existence which might otherwise have been prolonged to years of misery.

She had been unconscious, and her mind had been wandering for the past hour, but her husband's footfall, lightly though he trod, seemed to rouse her, and that wonderful interval of consciousness which the All-Merciful Being so frequently sends His dying creatures, ensued.

Having at her request been propped up in the bed with pillows, she clasped her husband's hand, and spoke with a difficult energy.

To upbraid him for his neglect of her? Not so.

"Darling!" whispered the loving wife, "I am dying; perhaps it is better so; I feel that I have been a burden to you, dearest; forgive me! I have been selfish and thoughtless; I loved you too much, darling; I tired you with my love, and drove you from me by my inability to hide my affection, and—and mine was but poor society for you, John, you who are so clever and so well educated; no wonder you found my conversation wearisome. Oh dearest! I see it all now! and had it been the will of God to spare my life, I could, I think, have been less selfish, less troublesome, less foolish! say you forgive me, darling?"

Little did the tender, innocent, simple girl

think what coals of fire she was heaping on her husband's head!

Which of them had been guilty of selfishness?

An impassioned kiss on the dry cracked lips of the dying woman was the only reply his feelings would permit.

"My child, my child!" continued the sufferer, "give me my child!" and the glazing eyes brightened, and the pale face was lit up with the ray of a mother's pride, as the nurse placed the little helpless squalling mass of humanity in her bosom.

The effort of speaking to her husband had been too much for her, and she sank back apparently exhausted; but suddenly raising herself again by an effort of which none could have believed her capable, she cried, "There! there! I see them all, father, mother, and Jacques, and—and—little Marie! Husband, dear! you remember little Marie! I am going to them! oh! so—so fast! Kiss me darling before you go, and—and you won't be

very late to-night, will you, dearest? 'Tis so,
so lonely, and—and John, dear! call her
Marie!"

> " The world recedes, it disappears!
> Heaven opens on my eyes! my ears
> With sounds seraphic ring!
> Lend, lend your wings! I mount! I fly
> O grave, where is thy victory?
> O death, where is thy sting?"

POPE.

CHAPTER II.

ALONE.

" Be taught, vain man ! how fleeting all thy joys,
    Thy boasted grandeur and thy glittering store ;
Death comes and all thy fancied bliss destroys,
    Quick as a dream it fades and is no more."
                                        BEATTIE.

THE young widower was known to his Parisian
acquaintances as John Brandreth: he had
been sent abroad as a young man to see a
little of the world and to acquire the conti-
nental languages. Whilst making a short stay
in the Channel Islands, he had fallen in love
with Lucy Geyton, the daughter of an hotel-
keeper in Guernsey, and, after a very short
courtship, had married her. Nor had she ever
given him cause to regret the step. Bran-

dreth knew well that his match would not be approved of by his parents, and being on a three years' tour, he thought it prudent to conceal from them as long as he could a union which he felt sure they would consider a *mes-alliance*. From his father, already an old man, he had great expectations, and as it was not at all improbable that his father might die before the termination of the three years' tour, he argued that it was far wiser for him to keep his secret than to publish the fact of his marriage at the risk of being disinherited. His wife's death now rendered it more than ever unnecessary for him to disclose the fact, and having placed the child out to nurse, he would be able to return to his home as he had left, " en garçon."

John Brandreth had led a reckless dissolute life, and had found Paris so fascinating that he had made it his abode for the last nine or ten months prior to his wife's death.

For more than an hour Brandreth knelt over the lifeless form, crushed by the sudden violence of the blow, and seeming scarcely to realize his position.

The old nurse, with a view to alleviate his distress, gently touched him on the shoulder, and called his attention to the child, which she had removed from the mother's bosom, and was dandling in her arms.

The sight of the child instantly brought to the widower's recollection the loss he had just sustained, and, with an impatient gesture, he thrust the old woman from him, ordering her to at once remove herself and the babe from his presence. It was no natural—or, to speak perhaps more correctly, unnatural—dislike of children, no innate brutality, that prompted Brandreth to act thus. There had been an exchange—the life of the wife for the life of the little child, and the bargain was terribly distasteful to him.

True it is that the birth of her child had cost Lucy her life, but equally true it is that her husband's thoughtlessness and neglect had reduced her to a state of weakness which could

ill bear the attendant sufferings. And Brandreth's conscience told him this; told him that
but for his conduct his wife would have had
strength to successfully combat her illness;
and therefore he sought to drown the whisper-
ings of that conscience by denouncing the babe
as the cause of the death of his darling.

He had been a gambler; night after night
had he left her alone: no complaint had ever
escaped her lips, but her wan face and sunken
eyes had too plainly testified how terribly she
felt her solitude. Brandreth had noticed the
change; noticed her careworn face, her wasting
form, and *pitied* her; but the demon of play
possessed him, and he had not the moral
courage to wrestle with the fiend. And now
retribution had come. *He* was alone now.

The unhappy man left the house, and walked
he hardly knew whither. After an hour's
walking he became more collected, and began
to reflect as to what course he should adopt.
He argued, as before, that his relatives being
unaware of his marriage, and his wife being

now dead, there could be no use in disclosing
to his family a secret which would probably
be displeasing to them. As for the child, he
determined to place it with some poor family
to bring up as their own, reserving to himself
the right of claiming it, should he feel inclined
hereafter to do so. With a heavy heart, and
an aching head, he returned to his lodging,
and in vain courted that fickle sleep which so
often refuses to visit us when we need it most.

On the following day John Brandreth gave
the necessary orders for his wife's funeral, and
then went in search of some lawyer to consult
as to the disposal of the child and her main-
tenance.

After walking some distance, he perceived
in the Rue Royale a brass-plate with the words
" Raimond, Notaire," and at once walked into
the lawyer's office.

He found the man of law intelligent, affa-
ble, and courteous, and had therefore no
trouble in getting at once to the business
which had induced him to seek legal advice.

Monsieur Raimond, who was a young man but a few years his senior, at once mastered the case, and saw at a glance Brandreth's anxiety to keep his marriage a secret, and to relieve himself of the burden thrust on him in the shape of the infant child.

On Brandreth's suggestion that the child should at once be put out to nurse, the lawyer shrugged his shoulders.

It was a good plan, an excellent plan, he said; but there would be difficulty. Did Monsieur know any person with whom the child could be placed? So far from knowing any one likely to take the child, Brandreth knew no one in Paris but a few dissolute young men who had been his companions at the gambling-tables.

The lawyer suggested that the medical man who attended Mrs Brandreth would be far more likely than any one else to know of some family where the baby could be placed; and on Brandreth's mentioning the doctor's name, Monsieur Raimond fell into an ecstasy

of delight : " Did he know the Doctor
Feuillet ? They were the best of friends. How
it was fortunate ! How it was extraordinary ! "
and the little fellow rubbed his hands and
seemed delighted. They would go and call
upon the Doctor Feuillet at once.

They proceeded at once to the doctor's residence, and found that gentleman at home.
Again it was fortunate—it was extraordinary !
On stating the object of their visit, Feuillet
informed them that he knew a woman, a
patient of his, who he expected would gladly
take care of the infant. She was the wife of
an artisan, and having known her for several
years past, he could confidently recommend
her as an honest industrious woman, and a
healthy wet-nurse.

Feuillet promised to call on his patient, and
consult her on the subject, and let Brandreth
know the result as soon as possible ; and, in
the event of her entertaining the proposal (and
of this he had little doubt) Brandreth and the
lawyer were to call upon the good woman, and

arrange as to terms. The latter gentleman, who was as kind-hearted as the doctor, and seemed already deeply interested in the affair, was delighted. " How it was fortunate ! How it was most fortunate ! Tout allait à merveille ! Il en était ravi ! " In such like expressions the little lawyer's feelings found vent.

The day after his wife's burial, Brandreth received a favourable communication from Doctor Feuillet, and accompanied by Monsieur Raimond, called on Madame Lejeune, the artisan's wife, whom they found precisely what Feuillet had described her. Her husband was a working jeweller by trade ; and, as they were poor, and had three young children, any small addition to their slender income would, she said, be most acceptable. The terms agreed on were that Brandreth should pay Madame Lejeune, through Raimond, twelve francs a week, and should be at liberty at any time to claim the child, and remove her from the Lejeune's custody. As twelve francs was a large weekly sum to pay for so young a child, it was further agreed that should Brandreth die before the girl became able to earn a living, the Lejeunes were not to expect any further payments from his estate. The object of this last arrangement was, of course, to ensure secrecy. The father was to provide money to buy an outfit of clothes and necessaries for his daughter.

Monsieur Raimond, as well as Dr Feuillet, in the absence of Brandreth, was to have access to the child to see that she was well cared for, and the bargain was struck.

The marriage certificate of Lucy Brandreth was handed over to the lawyer, and the widower, having left a sum of money in Raimond's hands to meet the weekly instalments payable to the Lejeunes, hurried away from Paris.

For ten or twelve years after his wife's death, Brandreth led a wandering life, travelling to and from the great capitals of Europe, vainly endeavouring to forget the cruel fact that, but for his own selfish and unfeeling

behaviour, the woman whom he had so dearly
loved, and whose value he had never discovered
until too late, might still have been his fond
wife and his child's mother.

CHAPTER III.

" Woman, the gift of heav'n, demands our love !
   On earth she constitutes our only bliss ;
   No undivided joy the soul can move,
    And Adam sighed alone in Paradise."
                     F. HODGSON.

OUR story demands that we should pass rapidly over the early life of little motherless Marie. From time to time Brandreth received news of the child through Monsieur Raimond. He had once or twice visited the Lejeunes to see her, but she, poor child, recognizing, of course, no other parents than her foster mother and her good husband, was terrified at the sight of a stranger, and rejected all the advances which Brandreth made towards her. Seeing no chance of winning the child's love, and how

happy she was with the Lejeunes, Brandreth
plainly perceived that he could not do better
than leave her where she was, and from that
time till Marie had attained the age of
eighteen he rarely saw her. A communication
of a most important nature from Monsieur
Raimond brought him to Paris soon after
Marie's eighteenth birthday. Pierre, the elder
son of the Lejeunes, who was then a fine-grown
young fellow of four and twenty, had proposed
marriage to Marie; the young people were
mutually attached to one another, the Lejeunes
were most anxious to secure at once the happiness of their son and their foster-daughter,
and nothing was wanting but Brandreth's sanction.

Marie had grown up a fine handsome girl,
and her father, on seeing her, deeply regretted
that he could not command the love of such a
daughter. With her intended, Brandreth was
much pleased ; but he felt that he should have
liked to have seen Marie allied to some man
a few rungs higher on the social ladder.

Pierre had, as a boy, been apprenticed to an owner of fishing-boats at the little village of Sante-Croix, on the coast of Normandy. His industry, honesty, sobriety and skill, had won for him the golden opinions of his employer, and at this early age he found himself in partnership with his old master, and part owner of three or four valuable fishing-boats and gear.

During the occasional visits which he made to his parents in Paris, the attachment which had existed between Marie and himself as children ripened into love, and finding the growing girl more beautiful and more amiable at each successive visit, he had now asked her to become his wife, and take care of a little house at Sante-Croix, which, in his mind's eye, he had already taken for her. Brandreth knowing that this alliance was, in a great measure, at least attributable to his own fault, and perceiving how deeply attached his daughter was to honest Pierre, concealed his disappointment, and gave his consent to the marriage, which was solemnized within ten days of his arrival in Paris, and very shortly afterwards the happy young folks took up their residence in the little house at Sante-Croix, and Pierre's fondest hopes were realised.

Brandreth was about to return to England, whence he had set out on receiving from the lawyer the intelligence of his daughter's attachment. The little doctor and Brandreth, and their mutual friend Raimond, were dining together at the house of the last, and were talking over the event which had just passed, and that which had occurred some eighteen years before.

Raimond and Feuillet were in great glee, the former especially.

"How it is fortunate!" said Raimond: "How it is extraordinary!"

The doctor was proud to think that the little girl *he* had brought into the world had grown up so strong, so healthy, so handsome, under the care of the woman whom *he* had recommended.

Both, of course, had been present at the wedding; indeed both had signed their names

in the Register Book as witnesses of the ceremony. Brandreth was not so elated; he felt,
truth to tell, somewhat ashamed of himself.
Of the· trio, he was the only one who had not
evinced the liveliest interest in the little Marie;
—he, her father. The tears gushed into his
eyes as he mentally compared the warm kiss
on both cheeks which the open-hearted innocent
girl had given Raimond and Feuillet on leaving
Paris, with the cold, formal salutation he had
himself received. He felt that as he had failed
to appreciate the mother's devotion, so had he
thrust aside the daughter's love.

Brandreth informed his companions, what
hitherto he had not divulged, that his father
was in a most precarious state, and that he was
heir-apparent to large landed property in England. At that present time, he observed, his
resources were limited; but on his coming into
the property he hoped to be able to make them
some fitting acknowledgment of their great
kindness to his daughter, his gratitude for which
he could not find words to express.

It would be necessary for him at once to return home, as it was hardly possible that his father could live many months. He promised to communicate with them, or one of them, from time to time, and expressed great contrition for his neglect of his daughter, for which he hoped to atone, by placing her and her husband in an independent state on his succeeding to his father's estates. At his death Marie would of course be his heiress, and he declared his intention of making Monsieur Raimond his executor

Both gentlemen thanked him for his kind intentions; but assured him that to have been of service to Marie was an ample reward for any trouble they might have taken. Monsieur Raimond here went to his escritoire, and produced a small bundle of papers, and, placing them in Brandreth's hands, said, "I trust you will pardon the liberty I have taken, but after Marie's birth you left Paris so hurriedly, that you omitted to leave any instructions as to the faith in which you wished her to be brought up. I therefore took upon myself to have her baptized, and some three or four years since she received, at the hands of the Bishop, the rite of confirmation and her first sacrament. She has been piously brought up, and educated by Madame Lejeune in the Roman Catholic faith; indeed, placed as she was with a family of that persuasion, it would have been most difficult, if not actually impossible, to instil into her any other doctrines. Here are your marriage certificate and Marie's certificate of baptism, and a copy of the register of her birth. I have taken office copies of them, and you had better take the originals into your custody."

Brandreth thanked Monsieur Raimond, and admitted that under the circumstances he could not have acted more wisely.

Doctor Feuillet also craved pardon for having, during Marie's youth, administered certain medicines to her, and attended her during one or two slight indispositions, without being authorized by Brandreth to do so.

Neither of these warm-hearted men would take one farthing for their professional services, and it was with a feeling of relief that Brandreth quitted them, for every little act of kindness they had done to his daughter reminded him too painfully of his own cruel conduct.

Raimond soon after received a letter from Brandreth, informing him of his safe arrival in D—— shire. The same letter informed him that his father had rallied in the most wonderful manner. Every year, at least, Raimond received intelligence of Brandreth, and the latter received, through Raimond, news of his daughter.

Two years after Brandreth's departure from Paris, the lawyer had a letter from him announcing his father's death and his succession to the property. In a letter written some months subsequently, however, Brandreth informed him that on taking possession he had found the estates so heavily incumbered that he foresaw there would, unless the most rigid economy were practised, be barely sufficient to pay the interest on the mortgages. Under

these circumstances he said it would be more
beneficial to Marie to apply the annuity which
he had intended for her towards paying off
these charges, so as to leave her at his death
an unincumbered estate, than to pay her the
money at that present time, as he had contem-
plated doing.   In this the lawyer fully agreed
with him; and in his reply to Brandreth's
letter expressed his condolence with him, re-
commending him to cut down his establishment,
and economise, as much as possible, so as to
free the estates the more quickly.   The letter
also contained a piece of news—Marie had
given birth to a daughter, and both were
doing well.

Some eight years after the birth of Brandreth's grand-daughter, Monsieur Raimond received a communication from D——shire, but
written by the valet of his old friend, informing
him that his master was so crippled with gout
that he was quite unable to use his right hand,
and from that time the letters to Raimond
were always written by this servant.

CHAPTER IV.

A MIGHTY NIMROD.

" Fill the bumper fair !
  Every drop we sprinkle
O'er the brow of care
  Smooths away a wrinkle.
Wit's electric flame
  Ne'er so swiftly passes,
As when through the frame
  It shoots from brimming glasses."

T. MOORF.

" 'GAD sir, I remember as if it were but yesterday, old Satyr taking me over the Park gate
—topped with most infernal spikes, just as it
is now—only wood in those days instead of
iron—five or six men had passed through,
when some lady of course let the gate shut
right in my face, sir ! Confound the women, I
say, what business have they in the hunting-
field ? none at all, sir ! out of place ! alto-

gether out of place! Well, you see, I had of
course been expecting the petticoat to give
the gate a swing, as any Christian would have
done. Devil a bit, sir! never even made an
attempt! old Satyr pulled up so short as
nearly to throw me over his head, and I was
righting myself in the saddle, when, by Jove,
sir, the old horse rose and bucked over the
gate standing — at a bound—you'd hardly
credit it, would you, Dick? That gate was
five feet high, sir, if it was an inch!"

The wine is with you, my boy.

" 'Gad, sir! I feel the old horse rising under
me now," continued Mr. Tyrrell, sitting well
back in his chair.

His companion thought that the port might
possibly have lent additional force to his
uncle's imagination, and that if he had used
the word " chair " instead of horse, he would
have been nearer the mark.

But Richard Tyrrell was a first-rate listener,
and knew better than to interrupt his uncle in
his after-dinner stories.

"That was a clipping run that day, I tell you, my boy! It was in the middle of the run that we ran through the park; old Satyr and I showed them the way from find to finish; and a brilliant finish it was too—rolled him over in the open on the top of White Down. One of the quickest things I ever rode in my life, sir," said the old gentleman, filling his glass.

"Now I don't say, mind you," continued he, "that I should *not* have ridden at the Park gate if the old nag had not taken me over before I intended; I don't say *that* mind you, my blood was up, and I don't think fixed bayonets would have stopped me then. I merely tell you the story as it happened, sir. Old Flint (he was the huntsman in those days; I am speaking of fifteen years ago, mind you), old Flint, I say, could scarcely believe that the old horse could have jumped a five feet six gate standing—'Gad sir, when the old gate was taken away, I had the new iron one of the very same height to commemorate the leap. I say,

Dick, six feet of spikes makes you shudder, don't it?"

The diplomatic nephew having given the shudder which his uncle's story demanded, and duly applauded the performance of the Satyr, began to sing the praises of the Port.

This young man was about twenty years of age. He was not of prepossessing appearance, nor was he one of his uncle's kidney, as he cared for no sort of field sport. He was a son of Mr. Walter Tyrrell, the younger brother of the sporting gentleman who took the extraordinary leap.

Walter Tyrrell had twice married, and this young man was the only child of the former marriage. The hunting season being over, and the guests who had been staying at Beechwood having taken their departure, Richard Tyrrell was staying for a few weeks with his uncle at Beechwood Hall.

John Tyrrell found, or thought he found, two or three redeeming points about his nephew. Firstly—He was a splendid listener, and never

wearied of his stories. Secondly—He always
drank fair. Richard Tyrrell hated the after-
dinner stories, and so far from drinking fair
drank half a bottle to his uncle's bottle and a
half. When his uncle's eye was upon him he
invariably finished his glass and re-filled to
the brim ; but, as we before observed, he was
very diplomatic, and Mr. Tyrrell generally
imbibed at least a pint more wine than he was
conscious of having done. One other recommendation had Richard ; he read well. He
used to read the *Times* after dinner to his uncle
until the latter went to sleep.

As John Tyrrell had no wife, an old housekeeper used to superintend the domestic economy of Beechwood Hall.

We have stated before that Richard was a
first-rate listener. It is not every one who is a
good listener, so far as after-dinner stories are
concerned.

When a man has reached his fifth lustre, and
has drank for fifteen or twenty years past, when
gout would permit, a bottle or more of port

a-day, however enthusiastic a sportsman he may
have been, depend upon it his performances are
better after dinner. And naturally so. The
seat cannot be so firm, the hand so light, the
eye so quick, the nerve so strong as of yore.
There is not the rapid circulation of blood
which youth enjoys, and what man can ride
boldly if he is cold? In short, our old sportsman shirks the fence and makes away for the
gate, and we ought to applaud his discretion.
This is in the field; but after dinner, when he
has well lined his stomach, and put himself
outside a bottle of generous port, seated by the
cheery fire-blaze, with his legs well under the
mahogany, instead of embracing the flanks of
his hunter, *then* the blood begins to circulate,
and how he does ride! We have known the
poor hobby almost ridden to death! We really
believe some of these jolly old bucks would ride
if we could get them into the saddle after-
dinner,—at all events we give them credit for
thinking they would. These after-dinner
romancers are a class " *sui generis.*" They are

most entertaining people, they are one of the stays of the dinner-table. Whether they are induced by their sporting zeal to imagine they really accomplished the marvels they narrate, whether they begin to believe them themselves from constant repetition, whether they tell them purely to amuse others, or in the hope of immortalizing themselves; how much is true, how much false, how many stories are founded on fact, and how many are without the slightest foundation, and lastly, whether the listeners are expected to believe all or any part of them— *c'est tout egal*—who cares? If the narrator believes the story he is relating, we cannot blame him; if he narrates what he knows to be false, we hope he does so merely to amuse his audience; and if he invents a good story as he goes on without tripping himself up, he shows himself a genius. Surely embellishment is a very venial crime.

To be a good listener a man must hear stories he has heard fifty times, as if he had never heard them before—he must never in-

terrupt, he must pass over any discrepancies;
should the story be inconsistent, he must fail
to see it, he must see nothing but the point,
and if there be no point (as not unfrequently
happens), he must pretend to see one, but he
must be careful to laugh at the right moment.
He should also betray astonishment, or any
other emotion that may be expected, and
occasionally ask where and when the event
occurred, so as to feign interest, and make
believe that the story is quite new to him.

Richard Tyrrell understood all this; he had
noticed how the wall had grown exactly one
foot during the story; he had also remarked
that although Mr. Tyrrell had followed six or
seven people in the middle of the run, he had
led the field from find to finish.

Richard's countenance never betrayed his
observations; he was a diplomatist. His father
might reasonably expect to succeed to Beechwood should he survive the present owner,
and was not he his father's eldest son?

In the midst of life we are in death; within

a week of relating the story of the Satyr, Mr.
Tyrrell came to an untimely end. His horse
had put his foot on a loose stone and fallen,
throwing his rider. Mr. Tyrrell was a heavy
man, and fell on his head. Concussion of the
brain was the result, and he died within four-
and-twenty hours of the accident.

The funeral over, the family lawyer announced that the late owner of Beechwood having died intestate, and without issue, the estate
passed to his brother Walter as heir-at-law.

Great surprise was expressed at a man
possessed of such large landed property having
left no will; but the statement was borne out
by Richard and the late Mr. Tyrrell's con-
fidental servant Filcher, who had searched
high and low, and declared that neither will,
nor even any paper containing any particular
wishes, could be found. The lawyer, Mr.
Hookham, felt aggrieved, as he doubtless
thought it a reflection on his advice; he,
however, was quite sure that had Mr. Tyrrell
been more provident, he would have had the

drawing of his will. He had frequently, he said, spoken to Mr. Tyrrell of the advisability of making his will, but the squire had always put the matter off.

Perhaps none regretted Mr. Tyrrell's death more than Filcher. " Poor dear master," said Filcher, " 'e was a gentleman, 'e was. I shan't never get another like 'un."

And Filcher spoke very feelingly. For ten years past he had enjoyed the run of the house, and, better still, of the cellar. For ten years he had had a snug billet. Acutely he felt the loss of his master; the consequent loss of the keys perhaps even more acutely.

" 'Tis 'ard," said he to Mrs. Crimp the housekeeper, " 'tis 'ard ; but there's One above will provide, M rs. Crimp. There's nothing more 'eavenly than 'ope, is there ma'am? Better myself I can't expect to; but, as we know, the Lord will provide."

When Mr. Walter Tyrrell took possession, Mr. Filcher got his congé. Mrs. Crimp was, however, retained as housekeeper.

CHAPTER V.

" His mother from the window look'd,
With all the longing of a mother."

LOGAN.

SEVEN years have elapsed since the death of Mr. John Tyrrell.

In the comfortably furnished drawing-room of Beechwood Hall, are seated four persons, two of either sex.

The elder gentleman is fifty-three years of age, but looks younger; rather above the middle height, and of very commanding and gentlemanly appearance; his features are regular, though not strictly handsome; the well-defined chin shows him to be a man of firmness; whilst his hair, as yet scarcely tinged with grey, and his fresh, healthy complexion, proclaim him a man who has lived a sober, steady, and methodical life.

This is Mr. Walter Tyrrell, the present owner of the Beechwood property, or, as he is more generally styled by his tenants, " the squire ; " he is sitting in his arm-chair reading the *Times* (by the way what would a country gentleman do without his *Times ?*), and the lady sitting at work in the recess of the bay-window is his wife. A young man of six or seven-and-twenty years of age is poring in-tently over the contents of the large volume be-fore him. No one can mistake him for a child of Mrs. Tyrrell, who appears too young to be his mother. This is Richard Tyrrell, whose acquaintance the reader made in the last chapter.

The present Mrs. Tyrrell's sweet counte-nance proclaims her to be what she is—a good and loving mother and a fond and duti-ful wife, whose happiness consists in making

all around her happy, and in superintending
the domestic economy of her establishment
with order and precision.

Rarely do we see a woman, the mother of
three children, whose features show no trace
of care or anxiety; but Mrs. Tyrrell's face is
as joyous, her hair as thick and long now as
on her wedding-day, between seventeen and
eighteen years ago. Her oval-shaped face
and eyes of the same rich brown tint as
her luxuriant hair, give a peculiar softness to
her expression. Her nose is straight, and
when she smiles (she nearly always wears a
smile) the dimples play round the little mouth,
and, but for her somewhat matronly figure, she
might pass for six or seven-and-twenty. No
one could look at her and believe her anything
but pure and virtuous.

On the stool on which her mother's little
arched feet are resting, sits a child of about
nine years of age, whom we cannot describe
better than by saying that she promises to
become Mrs. Tyrrell's counterpart.

The dissimilarity between the little girl and her half-brother Richard is very striking. His features, as we have said, are not prepossessing, and he is one of those persons to whom we somehow or other take an instinctive dislike, without being able to assign our reason for so doing.

> " I do not love thee, Doctor Fell,
> The reason why I cannot tell;
> But this alone I know full well,
> I do not love thee, Doctor Fell."

It was midsummer, and through the open windows the light breeze, gradually dying away with the sinking sun, stole in soft and balmy, loaded with the fragrant scent of the jasmine that clung to the front of the house.

From time to time Mrs. Tyrrell cast wistful glances towards the river, which ran at the foot of the slope on which the Hall is situate, and at last the object of her search came in view. A sweet smile, full of love and yearning, lit up her face as the snow-white canvass of the jib of a yacht of about twenty tons opened a point of the estuary about half a mile from the Hall.

"Here he is at last!" exclaimed Mrs. Tyrrell. "Look, Walter, how prettily the yacht glides along!"

Mr. Tyrrell came to the window, but did not appear so delighted with the scene as his better-half.

"Why, where on earth is the young madcap bringing her," said he; "he has passed the moorings by a quarter of a mile, she will ground if he is not very careful."

Presently "the Wild Duck" dropped her kellick and, bringing her sharp bow to the flood-tide, swung slowly round.

From the window could be seen a youth of sixteen, an old man very short and grizzled in appearance, and a diminutive urchin, who formed the crew, busily engaged in stowing the canvass and making all snug and ship-shape. Then the young gentleman, taking with him the small boy, cast off the punt which was astern, and pulled ashore. Directly the bow of the punt grated on the shingle, he neatly jerked his paddles in by a quick turn of the wrist, jumped over the gunwale, pushed her off, and before the boy had rowed back to the cutter, a distance of some thirty or forty yards, was half way up the lawn on his way to the Hall. Two or three minutes later he rushed somewhat unceremoniously into the drawing-room, threw his arms round his mother's neck, and kissed her affectionately. Mrs. Tyrrell said nothing, but one of her loving smiles passed over her face as she returned her son's caress.

"Why, Paul," said Mr. Tyrrell, "what made you bring the yacht so far up the creek, instead of leaving her at her moorings? You ran a great risk of sticking in the mud." "Oh, no, father!" cried Paul, "Old Bunt said there was plenty of water at spring-tides, and the tide was flowing, so I thought I might as well come by water as land. He will put the legs on her. Had rare sport," he continued, "a turbot, four brills, two or three

dories, and no end of whiting. Had a soldier's
wind, so we were able to run out to the fishing-
ground, and keep the trawl down for two or
three hours. Shrimp is going to bring up the
turbot and the brills when he has done his
work for old Bunt. Lovely day! there was
not roll enough to upset our little Nell," he
rattled on, stooping down and kissing the
little girl, who still sat on the stool at her
mother's feet. Here Richard Tyrrell, who knew
Paul's volubility, gave a look of intense disgust,
and, taking up the book in which he appeared so deeply interested, stole quietly from the
room.

The lad who had thus disturbed his re-
searches was a fine grown young fellow, neither
tall nor short for his age, but remarkably well-
proportioned and muscular.

His manly face was very much sunburnt,
and his hands were tanned of a colour approaching mahogany; his brown hair was very
thick and wavy, and a shade or so darker than
that of his mother; his eyes were of a greyish-

blue, and his prominent nose, if not actually large, was at least *bien prononcé;* it was, however, of a good Roman shape. His mouth was very small, too small perhaps for that of a boy, and was cut exactly like his mother's. It was pleasing to look upon his open countenance, beaming with health and happiness, in which respect his appearance differed greatly from that of his half-brother Richard, who not only looked sad and sullen, but delicate.

This might have been owing, in a great measure, to the widely different manner in which they spent their time, for they seemed to be diametrically opposed to each other in their habits, character, and pursuits. Paul was passionately fond of all kinds of sport, and seemed restless and uncomfortable to a degree when by any mischance he was confined to the house; Richard, on the other hand, cared little whether it rained or shone; he seldom went beyond the Park gates, and held Paul in contempt for deriving any pleasure from the pursuit of any kind of sport.

The two, therefore, saw but little of each other. Paul was between sixteen and seventeen years of age, and had just completed his last half at Eton, so he was now busily engaged in following up his favourite amusements.

Richard, though some ten years older than Paul, had not long finished his education; his passion for books easily overcoming the yearning which most young men evince to leave school.

For a man who not only disliked sporting himself, but was narrow-minded enough to despise others for so doing, Beechwood was perhaps as unsuitable a residence as could be; there was little or nothing for Richard to do but read, and read, read, read, he did; poor Richard seemed indeed a blighted being; his perpetual studies and sedentary habits had made him misanthropical to a degree.

He appeared to look upon his sweet stepmother as an intruder, although in his boyish days she had lavished her affection on him as on one of her own children; but Mrs. Tyrrell's

heart could not bear the contemptuous glance
which Richard was wont to throw on her
darling Paul on his return from his out-door
recreations.

CHAPTER VI.

BEECHWOOD.

" The house was a large square: but plain and low;
Wise Nature's use Art strove not to outgo."

COWLEY.

THE fine old estate of Beechwood comprises
about three thousand acres, and is admirably
adapted for the seat of a gentleman who is a
true lover of British sports. Hunting, shooting,
and fishing may be indulged in within easy
distance of the Hall, which stands in the centre
of about a hundred acres of park land enclosed
by a ring fence, and on which flourish some
remarkably fine-grown old trees, which probably
gave their name to the estate. The Hall itself
is built in the Elizabethan style, a large house

built for comfort rather than show. The walls
are of great thickness, and the whole fabric
wears an appearance of massiveness and solidity.
In front of the house the lawn slopes gradually
downwards for nearly a quarter of a mile, and
at the foot of the hill flows a small river, the
waters of which meet the tide at high water at
this point. Within half a mile or less from
the junction of the fresh and salt waters, the
bed of the river widens very suddenly, forming
an estuary which gradually increases in breadth
towards the mouth of the river, which may be
perhaps a quarter of a mile across. Although
small until entering the Beechwocd estate, the
river below its junction with the tidal waters is
navigable to small craft up to within less than
half a mile of the Hall, while a similar distance
above the confluence finds it a trout stream,
clear as crystal, and extremely rapid in its
course, until arrested in the impetuosity of its
career by the widening of its bed on nearing
the sea. At the head of the estuary a bend in
the river's course secures shelter and a snug

anchorage for Mr. Tyrrell's little yacht and two or three hookers belonging to the fishermen of the little village of D——. The navigation of the stream is, it is true, somewhat difficult on account of its windings; but this objection is more than counterbalanced by the protection which the serpentine character of the creek affords to the boats, which, if the river ran in a direct line to the coast, would be exposed to the gales from the sea. Beechwood is indeed a paradise for a sportsman.

A yacht lying snugly at her moorings within sight of the windows—hounds—hunted regularly within easy distance—fresh and salt water fishing—shooting of the most varied description, the estate fairly stocked with game, and wild fowl of many sorts frequenting the creek and neighbouring marshes in the cold weather; with a suitable income, what more does a human being want?

CHAPTER VII.

ANNETTE.

" And ne'er did Grecian chisel trace
  A Nymph, a Haiad, or a Grace,
  Of finer form or lovelier face !
  What though the sun, with ardent frown,
  Had slightly tinged her cheek with brown—
  The sportive toil, which, short and light,
  Had dyed her glowing hue so bright,
  Served too in hastier swell to show
  Short glimpses of a breast of snow."

WALTER SCOTT.

WE must pass over two years, and take a look at our old friends the Lejeunes. The summer was over, the leaves were beginning to fall, and the days were shortening rapidly. The wind howled dismally in the old-fashioned chimney of a small house, which stood, and perhaps still stands, in the main

street of a little seaport town on the wild coast
of Normandy.

In the principal room of this house were
seated a woman of about thirty-eight, and two
strikingly handsome girls of eighteen and
fifteen respectively ; Madame Pierre Lejeune
and her daughters, Annette and Christine.
The former was busily engaged in knitting a
coarse woollen jersey, evidently intended for
some fisherman. The elder girl was tall and
beautifully proportioned, and her dark brown
hair was coiled round and round in a simple
twist, and fastened at the back of the
classically-shaped head by a tortoise-shell
comb. Seated on a low chair close to the
hearth, on which a small wood fire was
burning, her hands clasping her knees, her
large blue eyes fixed on the embers, she
appeared to be listening to the moaning of
the wind, and to the dull monotonous sound
caused by the dashing of the waves against the
rocks of the iron-bound coast, which every now
and then struck upon the ears of the inmates

of the room like distant thunder. She had not
the features of a French peasant—her face
exhibited none of the coarseness which usually
characterizes the race. The straight Grecian
nose and delicately-cut nostrils seemed to
assert gentleness of birth ; the short upper lip
betrayed something of pride, but the fulness
of the lower, and the pretty curve of the little
mouth, entirely contradicted any insinuations
against her temper. The expression was somewhat haughty, but very sweet, for although the
features were decided, there was not a hard
line in her loving, innocent face. The coarse
blue serge frock in which she was attired, did
not in the least detract from her beauty ; its
extreme simplicity perhaps suited her better
than a more fashionable garment would have
done.

She was at length aroused from the reverie
in which she had been indulging, by her mother
exclaiming, as a squall, more angry than the
previous ones, struck the old house, " The Bon
Dieu preserve us, what a night ! And your

father not yet returned! Go, Annette, ma
chère, run down to the quay and see if the
boats are in. The sun must have set these two
hours, the night is dark as pitch, and it is
blowing hard on shore. I wish your father were
home." As soon as the girl had set off on her
errand, Madame Lejeune proceeded to rake
together the wood embers, and by the aid of a
pair of bellows and a fresh log, soon procured a
bright clear fire. Annette had not been gone
more than ten minutes before she returned,
saying that her father had arrived, and would
be home shortly; he was merely lending a
hand to pack the fish and moor the boat
securely for the night. "Father is cold and
wet," said she; "he will be glad of his supper
and dry clothes as soon as he comes."

Having made some coffee, Annette laid a
coarse but scrupulously clean cloth on the
deal table, and produced from a cupboard
some black bread, a piece of pork, and a small
bottle of brandy.

These arrangements for the evening meal

were just completed, when a man, apparently some forty years of age, entered. Having thrown off the dripping tarpaulins with which he was almost entirely covered, he approached his wife and daughters, and kissed them affectionately. Annette wrung the briny water from her father's beard, exclaiming, "pauvre petit papa, voilà votre soupé, mangez bien, petit papa." The adjective could only have been used by Annette in an endearing sense, as her "petit papa" stood about five feet eleven without his long sea boots, and was broad-shouldered in proportion. He had a handsome manly countenance, and was like his daughter in feature.

The reader will, doubtless, have recognized Madame Lejeune as the daughter of Brandreth, and the wife of Pierre.

Annette spoke French with a Parisian accent. She owed the accuracy of her pronunciation to a Madame Lorin, who resided in a chateau about two miles from Sainte-Croix. This lady had taken a great fancy to the fisherman's little girl, and Annette from her childhood had been constantly in the society of Madame Lorin and her daughter Julie.

The latter was much about her own age, and Madame Lorin kindly allowed Annette to take lessons in English singing and music from the masters who came to instruct her own daughter, and thus our heroine received a much more elaborate education than would otherwise have fallen to her lot. These great advantages were not lost upon Annette, who was naturally clever, and notwithstanding lessons sometimes missed by her absence, owing to stress of weather, or in consequence of her being required at home, she was at least as good a scholar as Julie, and far surpassed her fellow-pupil in music. Her voice, too, naturally sweet and of great range, developed wonderfully under the tuition of an able master, and Madame Lorin's love of music rendered the girl's society very pleasant to her.

Annette's position with regard to Julie

Lorin was almost that of a foster-sister, for there was so little society in the vicinity of Sainte-Croix, that Madame Lorin was glad to have her as a companion for her own daughter, notwithstanding the difference in their rank. But Annette had grown up "every inch a lady," thanks to Madame Lorin's kindness in educating her; and if poverty be no crime, Mademoiselle Lejeune had little to be ashamed of.

The good widow Lorin had one son, Henri, the pride of his mother's heart. He was a subaltern in the army, a fine, well-grown, handsome lad of twenty; and had been for some time at home on sick-leave, but was now convalescent. During his illness Annette, glad of an opportunity of showing her gratitude to her benefactress, had nursed him with great care and kindness; can it be wondered that the vivacious young officer's society pleased the simple and confiding young girl? Alas! those pretty speeches and compliments which go for nothing with the ball-going young

lady, tell most cruelly on an innocent girl in
Annette's position. How could she fail to be
pleased and flattered at the attentions paid
her by a good-looking young officer? she who
had scarcely ever seen a young man of Henri's
stamp before? For seven or eight months had
Henri been at home, and now the time of
his departure was at hand; a time to which
Annette looked forward with much sorrow, for
she felt that she loved, and would have died for
him.

In his mother's presence Henri paid her no
attentions, and she was glad of this, for her
modest nature would have shrunk from receiving them except when alone with him.
Unsophisticated as she was, she attributed
this reserve to modesty; for the poor girl used
to blush like a peony when Madame detected
her tender glances towards her son, and she
measured Henri by her own standard. Madame Lorin could not help observing the
girl's embarrassment, and suspected that poor
Annette was dazzled by the handsome features

and polished bearing of her soldier-boy, but as she had no reason to believe that Henri loved her protegée, she attached little or no importance to the matter, hoping that Henri's absence would quickly efface the impressions, if any, left upon the girl. Henri himself had suddenly discovered that it was important that he should at once rejoin his regiment, and his departure was therefore to take place at once.

CHAPTER VIII.

UNREQUITED AFFECTION.

" Or if (ah, too faithful!) with fondness she sighs
For one who has ceased her affection to prize,
Forgetting the vows by whose magic he strove
To gain that rich treasure, the virgin's first love.

. . . .

" If, tempted by interest, he venture to shun
The gentle affection his tenderness won;
Through passion's soft maze with another to rove,
Where then the delight of the virgin's first love ? "

OPIE.

By the pale moonlight may be seen two figures in the extensive garden of the chateau in which Madame Lorin resided. It is about seven o'clock in the evening, and the month is December, and Henri Lorin and Annette Lejeune are walking side by side down a path in the shrubbery, at a little distance from the chateau.

The girl's face is deadly pale, and appears almost ghastly by the sickly light of the moon; the man's features are firmly set, and a contemptuous smile curls his upper lip, as he suddenly stops, and confronting her, exclaims in a scornful tone—

"Vous plaisantez, ma chère! You surely could never have thought so. Marry you! Do you take me for a fool?"

Annette said nothing, but the nervous twitching of her blanched lips, and the heaving of her bosom, too plainly told of the bitter pangs which were piercing her tender heart; her head swam, and a feeling of sickness came over her. She tottered, and would have fallen had not the young man caught her and drawn her arm through his own. With an effort of which one would scarcely have thought her capable, the unhappy girl tore herself away, and leant against the trunk of a small tree at a few paces from Lorin.

"Henri," said she, "how can you dare speak to me thus? You do not know—you cannot

know—how I have loved you. Have not I
done everything in my power to please you?
And now you are going away on foreign service
for years—perhaps I may never see you again!"
Her sobs prevented her saying more, and with
an hysterical laugh, she fell to the ground.
Lorin raised her, unhooked the bosom of her
dress, and held his pocket-handkerchief, which
was scented with *eau-de-cologne*, to her nostrils.
After a few minutes she recovered from her
insensibility, and Lorin, in a kindlier tone,
endeavoured to calm her, and reason away her
grief. Annette listened attentively to him without replying, but her lovely face betrayed the
convulsions which were at work within her.
There was a pause for two or three minutes,
during which time the poor girl appeared ab-
sorbed in deep thought.

Love was getting the better of her pride,
and, in a faltering voice, she exclaimed, " Forgive me, Henri; I was wrong. I was selfish to
expect such a thing; but little did I think of
our parting. No, no! Henri, dear, we need

not part; you will take your little Annette with you as your servant—as anything—as anybody, only let me be near you to share your dangers, to nurse you when ill, to make you happy and comfortable when well, to work for you, to die for you! How could I be so vain as to expect you to marry the daughter of a poor fisherman? How could I be so ungrateful as to entertain any such idea, which must be displeasing to your mother, my friend and benefactress? You will do this, Henri, dear?" and Annette pressed her lips to his passionately.

Lorin's face became cloudy, and he reflected for an instant before answering her. He had not bargained for this; he had not believed any love could be so intense. He was, however, too accomplished a villain to let the girl perceive his embarrassment, and, whilst embracing Annette warmly, he bethought him how best he could avert the new calamity which threatened him.

"Annette, dear," said he, "you know what

pain it will cost me to part with you. Are you the only sufferer? My duty calls me away, and would to heaven that it were possible for you to go with me; but what you ask is madness; your flight at the time of my departure would create suspicions. How would your absence be accounted for? If you love me, as you say you do, you will not ask me to take a step which would break the heart of my mother, your benefactress. Do you not see that your disappearance from here would be immediately associated with my departure; and have I not already told you that it would break my mother's heart if she knew in what relation we stand to one another? Besides, your father and mother, child; you forget them. You love your parents, I suppose?"

"Love them? yes! at least I thought I did until;—until—my God. Henri! what are father and mother to me now!" said Annette, sobbing. Lorin started. "I thought, Annette," said he, assuming a reproachful tone, " you were a dutiful girl—you have often told me

how tenderly you loved your parents, and now
to gratify your selfish whims you ask me to
inflict on them this heavy blow, this fearful
anxiety!"

"God forgive me! Henri, I do ask you, and
if you refuse me, I will follow you wherever you
may go."

"Listen! Annette," said the young man
after a momentary pause, "in less than a year
I shall be enabled to get leave of absence for a
short time, I will then return and entreat my
mother to consent to our union, on condition
that you remain quietly here until my return,
and tell nothing of what has passed between us
to a living creature. Should you break either
of these conditions, I will not redeem my
promise."

Annette's eyes brightened whilst he was
speaking. "Oh Henri," said she, "I could
reconcile myself to any terms for the chance
of gaining such a prize as you. Do you think
there is any chance of Madame Lorin's giving
her consent?"

" That will depend mainly on your behaviour to her during my absence," returned Lorin.

There was a pause of some moments; the cheering promises held out by Henri had brought the colour to Annette's cheek again. Lorin broke the silence, and taking the girl's hand, said, " Is it a bargain, Annette ? "

" It is," replied the girl.

" Are you certain," continued Lorin, " that no one suspects anything ? "

" Quite certain," said she.

And stooping down he whispered something in her ear. Annette blushed painfully at the question he had put to her; but turning her head and looking towards the ground, she said, " No, there is no cause to fear that."

" God be praised," exclaimed Henri in a sincere tone, feeling relieved to find there was no risk of his conduct being discovered.

" After all your case is not nearly so bad as it might have been."

" Perhaps so," returned the girl with a sigh; " but I could almost wish it were otherwise.

Twelve long months! Oh, Henri, those months will appear years, and if I knew that I were to become the mother of your child, the thought would cheer my lonely hours."

" Bah, child," said Henri, " your chance of ever becoming my wife would be small indeed were that the case. Do you think my mother would receive you then as now ? "

" Is it a crime to love ? " returned Annette, simply.

" *Ma foi,* no ! " answered the young man ; " but it is a great sin to be found out."

" You will often write to me, Henri ? " asked the girl.

" Of course," replied he quickly, " and now Annette I must bid you good-bye.

" But Henri, dear, I shall see you again to-morrow ? "

" No ; although I shall not start until the day after, I shall be occupied all to-morrow in making the necessary arrangements for my departure ; besides, we may have no other opportunity of taking an affectionate farewell."

The young girl threw herself upon him, and clasping his neck with her arms, pressed her lips passionately to his.

" You will not betray me, Annette ? " said Henri, looking straight into the upturned face, as if to satisfy himself as to her sincerity.

" Never whilst you live," replied the girl, readily.

" Swear it ! " exclaimed the young man.

" I swear it ! " repeated the girl, slowly.

" Well, well, good-bye, Annette ; twelve months will soon slip away," said Henri, in a gay tone.

• " Kiss me once more, darling," whispered the trembling girl; and again the loving arms were twined round the worthless object of her adoration.

" God bless and preserve you, Henri dear, and grant you a speedy return," sobbed Annette, mastering bravely the emotion she felt, " you will come back as soon as possible to your poor girl ? "

" Yes, yes," said the soldier, " cheer up child,

and remember your oath ; " and after kissing the cold cheek he gently disengaged himself from the girl's embrace, and sauntered slowly towards the house.

He had not proceeded many yards before he heard a light step behind him, and Annette's quivering voice, saying, "Henri, dearest Henri," say " God bless you, Annette ! "

" There, there, God bless you, child," said he in an impatient tone, and avoiding the threatened caress, resumed his walk towards the château.

Annette Lejune walked slowly back to her home in the little narrow street, feeling as only a woman who has parted with the object of her love can feel, and through the long weary sleepless night the coarse linen of her pillow was bedewed with her tears.

CHAPTER IX.

THE STORM.

" But who shall bide Thy tempest ? who shall face
The blast that wakes the fury of the sea ?
Oh God! "

W. C. BRYANT.

THREE months had elapsed since Henri Lorin's departure, and no news of him had reached Annette, except through the château.

Day after day passed slowly, steadily on, but no letter from Henri. Madame Lorin and Julie had received letters informing them of his arrival at his destination, and of his good health, and in these epistles he sent his "kind regards" to Annette.

His "kind regards" to the woman that

would have died for him! Annette's heart ached, but no feeling of resentment or mistrust arose in that sincere, loving girl. "He is trying me," she would repeat to herself, "to see how true I can be to him."

"Petit papa," her mother, and Madame Lorin, could not imagine the cause of Annette's loss of spirits and appetite, and the honest fisherman, under pretence of requiring her services in his boat, often beguiled her to accompany him as the spring of the year came on, hoping that the open air might restore the health of his daughter; and these excursions seemed certainly beneficial to her. Her colour and appetite partially returned, but she was unhappy, very unhappy, although she battled bravely against her affliction. Summer passed, autumn came.

On a wild night the Lejeunes, father, mother, and daughters were seated in the little room where the reader first made the acquaintance of Annette and her sister. A fierce, equinoctial gale was raging without, the wind

howled dismally in the great chimney, and the
rain pattered against the small windows.

"Petit papa" was engaged in repairing some
fishing gear; Madame Lejeune was occupied as
usual with her knitting; whilst Annette sat
in a low chair moody and disconsolate. Need
it be told of whom she was thinking? Suddenly
a loud report shook the walls of the cottage.
A second convinced the inmates that the
sounds were not thunder-claps. The loud
booming at regular intervals was understood
by the fisherman; they were minute guns;
"A vessel in distress!" exclaimed Pierre,
throwing aside his fishing-gear and snatching
up his tarpaulin garments; "God help the
poor fellows aboard her!" Pierre was soon on
the quay, where most of the inhabitants of
Sainte-Croix now stood in a state of fearful excitement. The night was cloudy and
very dark, but soon a vivid flash of lightning
discovered a large vessel apparently at the
mercy of the wind and waves. Flash after
flash revealed her position for an instant,

and after every flash she was again lost in the
pitchy darkness. The flash of her guns, however, indicated at intervals her whereabouts.
She seemed to be about four miles from the
shore, towards which she was fast drifting. It
was evident that she must go ashore. She was
embayed, and could make no headway against
the gale. " There is only one chance for her,"
cried Pierre, " to board her and run her in
over the bar ; if she strikes on the bar there
is better hope of saving life than if she runs on
the rocks. It is close upon high water, and if
she is run fast on the sand, the tide will leave
her if she holds together for an hour's ebb. I
fear so large a vessel can never float over the
bar, but we cannot tell what water she may
draw ; it is her only chance. Comrades, you
will not stand by and see fellow-creatures
perish without an effort to save them ? Who
mans my lugger ? I shall want extra hands."
Three or four fishermen volunteered ; many,
however, shook their heads, declaring it would
be madness to attempt to board the vessel on

such a night. "Let me go, father," whispered Annette, who had just reached Pierre's side. "You shall take the helm, my lass," said Pierre, divesting himself of his over-all, and wrapping it round his daughter.

The entrance to the little harbour of Sainte-Croix was the mouth of a small river. A formidable bar of sand extended three-fourths of the width of the river's mouth, leaving but a very narrow and winding channel for craft to pass through. To beat the lugger out in the teeth of such a gale through such a narrow channel required no ordinary skill. There was plenty of water for the little craft over the bar at this time of the tide, but an on-shore gale raised such a surf in the shallow water, that nothing but a life-boat could live in it. Hence the necessity for keeping the channel, where, owing to the greater depth the water was comparatively smooth.

In a few minutes the fishing-boat was bounding along under a try-sail and a little rag of a storm-jib, quite as much, however, as she could stagger under. So fierce was the wind that the raindrops beat like hail, making Annette's face smart as she steered the boat on her errand of mercy. The people on the quay could not see the lugger, but they could see her lantern, now riding on the top of a wave, now dipping into the trough of the sea. They could hear every now and then the loud flapping of her sails as Annette, at her father's command, put her about. On one hand a rocky shore, on the other a seething mass of white broken water— to miss stays here were bad indeed. Pierre stood forward and trimmed the little jib as he shouted, "Hard a lee!" to his daughter. It was hard work for Annette, and took some strength to tend the tiller. With firm hands, and on the *qui vive* for the word of command, the brave girl coaxed the lugger to windward, taking advantage of every gust to keep her luff, and never letting her fall away. The gentle flip-flap of the foot of the trysail told her to a nicety that the sails were full but that the boat could lie no closer. They had now

reached the open sea, and the drenching spray
came right aft as every now and then a heavy
sea would break over the weather-bow, making
the lugger shiver from stem to stern. The
crew of the vessel had seen the lugger's light,
and knowing that a boat had put off to their
assistance, kept burning blue lights and flares-
up, to show their whereabouts, and give light
to those on board the lugger.

She was a large full-rigged ship ; her after
canvass had been blown away, and her hawsers
had apparently just parted, as she was drifting
stern first to her doom. A minute or two
more and she would drift past them. Pierre
had fastened one end of a long line round
his waist, and now stood ready to throw the
coil of the other end on board the ship.
" Hard down, lass," shouted he, and the lugger
immediately shot up in the wind's eye, and was
laid-to within two or three fathoms of the
passing ship. Quick as thought, and with
wonderful dexterity, the fisherman threw the
line aboard, shouted to the crew to make their

end fast, and haul him on board, and the instant he felt the line tauten, plunged into the angry sea. For a few moments Annette held her breath in fearful suspense, and great was her relief when, by the aid of a ghastly blue light, she saw her father drawn up over the side of the vessel. Pierre safe on board, Annette put about her little craft, which, with eased sheets, was soon bounding back past the disabled vessel towards the shelter of Sainte-Croix.

The ship which Pierre had thus courage-ously boarded was a transport, with a number of sick and time-expired soldiers on board. The most dreadful confusion prevailed, and the majority of those aboard were in despair. The captain inquired eagerly of Pierre what harbour there was, and what could be done for the safety of the ship and her living freight. "Leave all to me," said Pierre, "and, with God's help, I may save many lives. We must cant her. Can you make any sail on her for-ward?" The after-sails having been carried

away, the head-sails of the transport had been
taken in. An outer-jib was now, however,
quickly run up, and taking advantage of the
vessel's stern way, Pierre soon canted her, and
stood straight in for the sand-bar, now scarcely
a mile distant. "What water do you draw?"
asked Pierre of the captain. "Eighteen feet
at least," was the reply. The fisherman knew
at once it was hopeless to attempt to get the
ship into the little port; he, therefore, resolved
to run her aground on the bar as near the
shore as he dare. More canvass was now put
on the vessel to give her better steerage-way,
and to run her the faster upon the sand. As
the water became more shallow, the surf became terrific, and more than once the ship was
nearly pooped. Happily for the poor creatures
on board, the darkness prevented their seeing
the terrible seas that broke over the bar. All
on deck prepared themselves for the momenta-
rily expected shock. The suspense was awful,
and moments seemed hours. Would she never
strike? Some began to hope that Pierre had

miscalculated the depth of water, and that the ship would float over the bar. Not so the experienced fisherman who watched the shiftings of the sand after every spring tide. "Stand by!" shouted Pierre, at the top of his voice, "the next sea will put her ashore! Hold on for your lives!" Another moment and a terrific shock shook the vessel from end to end; the receding sea rushed back on either side, leaving the transport hard aground. The sea now broke completely over the vessel, sweeping her decks from stern to bow. Many of the crew had betaken themselves to the rigging, whilst others had got as far forward as possible to avoid the seas which kept break-ing over the stern. Nothing more could be done until the tide went back. Meanwhile those on shore were busily preparing a basket apparatus for taking off the men. Directly the tide had ebbed sufficiently to admit of the attempt, Pierre was hard at work endeavouring to establish the basket communication between the ship and the shore. For this purpose he had climbed to the main-top, and was securing the end of the line which was to be sent ashore, when the standing rigging suddenly gave way, and the mainmast went by the board, hurling Pierre and two seamen who were assisting him into the raging surf, and killing or wounding in its fall several of those on deck.

CHAPTER X.

" Air slumbers; wave with wave no longer strives,
    Only a heaving of the deep survives,
    A tell-tale motion!   Soon it will be laid,
    And by the tide alone the water sway'd."
                                        WORDSWORTH.

AFTER a storm comes a calm. The following
morning broke bright and clear on the scene of
the horrors of the previous night. The wind
had quite gone down, the sun shone warmly,
the sea had subsided, leaving a long rolling
ground swell. On the bar, however, was con-
clusive evidence of the anger of the elements.
The wreck of the once noble vessel lay fast
embedded in her sandy resting-place, her main
and mizen-masts hung over her side, her bul-

VOL. I.   G

warks were smashed in, she had opened in several places, and would probably soon go to pieces. Happily, however, she had held together until daylight, when, by the aid of the basket apparatus, the women and children had been taken off. A small line had been thrown ashore from the vessel by a rocket, and to this line was attached a hawser, which was hauled on shore by those on the rocks, the shore end of the hawser being made fast, whilst the other was firmly secured to the foretop of the ship. By the time the women and children were all taken off, the danger of further loss of life was at an end. The sea had run down sufficiently to admit of boats coming alongside, and many of the perishable articles were got out before the re-approach of high water.

The fall of the main-mast had been the only fatality. Nothing had as yet been seen of the bodies of Pierre and the two sailors who were precipitated from the main-top. Several persons had been injured or knocked overboard by the fall of the mast and two killed, the bodies of these latter were brought ashore and laid out in a room in the village cabaret.

Prompted by that morbid curiosity which characterizes the class, the poor inhabitants of Sainte-Croix crowded into the little room to get a glimpse of the dead. Their features were, however, quite unknown to them.

Through the entire night of the wreck, the Lejeunes, mother and daughters, had remained on the rocks watching the ill-fated vessel, dreading every moment lest she should go to pieces, and fearfully apprehensive for the safety of the brave fisherman. And when the morning broke, and the tide receded, and the seas broke less violently over the vessel, what heart-felt thanks they gave to their God! Little thought they that the spirit of him that was most dear to them, their all in all, had flown! But so it was, and when the sad news was brought ashore, what grief was theirs!

Towards mid-day a rumour reached the Lejeunes that a body had been recovered. They hurried to the spot, where a knot of people had already collected. It would be, they felt, some consolation to recover the body and imprint a last kiss on that well-loved face. Alas! it was not the body of Pierre. On a rude stretcher formed of a boat's bottom-boards hastily put together, lay a young man in undress uniform. The features were slightly mutilated, and the deceased had evidently been struck across the head by the falling gear and knocked overboard. For an instant Annette gazed intently on the distorted face, a giddiness came over her, and without sound or gesture she fell senseless on the prostrate form. She had recognized the body as that of Henri Lorin. On closer examination, her mother, sister, and several of the villagers assured themselves that it was indeed no other than he, and the terrible news was quickly on its way to the chateau. The conduct of Annette had created a little surprise amongst the bystanders, who, however, imagined that this second fatality had been too much for her nerves, already unstrung by the loss of her father. Moreover, they had no time

to wonder on this eventful day, and this little
episode was soon forgotten, and merged in the
great catastrophe. Grief reigned supreme at
Sainte-Croix. Pierre had been loved and re-
spected by all the inhabitants, and having received a better education than those around
him, he had always been looked upon as an
authority. What a change had one wild night
wrought on the little cottage, where but a few
short hours before all seemed so prosperous !
What had so short a time before been a happy
home, had now become but a refuge for the
fatherless and widow.

We will not dwell on the grief of these poor
creatures, or the weary anxious hours spent in
searching for the body. Suffice it to say, that
it was after two or three days recovered, and
was buried in the little chapelyard, whither the
whole population of Sainte-Croix mournfully
followed it. Three other bodies were consigned
to the earth at the same time; those of the
two men killed by the mast, and that of Henri
Lorin. Strange fate! On that terrible night

Annette lost her best friend and her worst enemy, and the remains of the brave man and the cowardly betrayer of his daughter lie peacefully side by side.

The wrecked vessel proved to be a French government transport bound for Cherbourg. Lorin finding the climate of a hot country beginning to tell on him, had just effected an exchange into a home regiment, which he was on his way to join.   On nearing his destination the storm came on, and by a singular coincidence, the vessel was run aground almost within sight of his own home, and that of the girl he had so cruelly wronged.

CHAPTER XI.

" For every inch that is not fool is rogue."

DRYDEN.

IN the spring of the second year from the occurrence of the events narrated in the last chapter, Richard Tyrrell was sitting one day in his sanctum at Beechwood, when a note was brought him. Hastily glancing over the contents, he dismissed the servant, and putting on his hat walked hastily towards the Park gate, where he was met by a seedy-looking individual.

" Well, Filcher, what's in the wind now? " began Richard, with an uncomfortable look. " Well, sir, the fact is I am off on a bit of

a cruise, going to do a little yachting."
Richard felt relieved. "I have got a situation as valet to Mr. Witney, the owner of the
schooner "Zouave," perhaps you may have
heard of her; so, as we may be away twelve
months or so, I thought I should like to see
you before starting."

"Very kind, very considerate, indeed,
Filcher," said Richard, "I congratulate you
on having secured such a capital situation;
Witney has money." Filcher looked grave.

"Ah, Mr. Richard, many of those as 'as it
don't know how to do good with it! Lord,
sir, if you 'ad his money what a power of good
you would do amongst us poor!" Richard
winced; he guessed what was coming. "This
hout-fittings a monstrous expensive job," continued Filcher, "when one goes to take a situation like this 'ere, one must go decent."

"Of course, of course," replied Richard;
"and if a five pound note is any use to you,
Filcher."

"Three fives, Mr. Richard, if you please,"

suggested Filcher, insinuatingly. And three fives it was eventually. After the receipt of the money Filcher soon withdrew, and proceeded towards the town to make his purchases preparatory to joining "The Zouave."

Three or four days after a magnificent yacht of 150 tons might have been seen gliding rapidly out of Ryde harbour before a northerly breeze. Let us see who are on board.

There is the owner, George Witney, a pale enervated young man, the only son of a tailor who died some two years since, leaving him an immense fortune. He is about seven or eight-and-twenty, and is taking seemingly as much pains to get rid of his money as his parent did to amass it.

On this occasion he has with him but one companion, Captain Leach, late of the —— th. The captain is a constant attendant on Witney, a sort of guardian angel in fact. The captain has little or nothing beyond his half-pay to live on, and he therefore finds it extremely comfortable and convenient to accept Witney's hospitality, although his friend's father was a tailor. The captain was above such vulgar prejudice ; but, at the same time, he loved to patronise the young man, so far as he could do so without damage to his own interests. Leach was some ten or twelve years older than Witney. He had been in a cavalry regiment, from which he retired, when retiring became the only step which saved him from being kicked out. Certain little irregularities in his accounts, and mistakes affecting the score at various games of chance, rendered it desirable that the ——th should know him no more. Since quitting the regiment, he had lived principally by his wits, and never had he been in such clover as now that he had the luck to fall in with George Witney. He was a cool calculating fellow enough naturally, but years of idleness, late hours, and bad company, had set their mark on him, and his passion for strong drink often got the better of his judgment.

The skipper of the yacht was an intelligent man of the name of Phillips, and he had for mate Jem Marline, a young man of six or seven-and twenty, who having served his apprenticeship in a western pilot-boat, had deservedly earned the reputation of a smart young sailor. There were besides these the cook and steward, making with the eight other hands a complement of twelve, exclusive of Filcher, who had little or nothing to do but attend on the persons of the captain and Witney. These worthies had started off on a cruise they hardly knew whither.

The captain was continually pointing out to his friend the necessity of being master of his own ship, to take the crew on the "ground hop," as he put it. "There isn't one yachtsman in a hundred," Leach would remark, "that is master aboard his own ship, these fellows of skippers have it all their own way. Now look you here, George, my boy, we'll show them who's master here."

Now, the captain was right enough, and Witney would have been right to show that he was not to be imposed upon, but unfortunately he could not make the crew understand his sentiments in an unoffensive manner. This petty despotism pleased Witney, as it made him feel important, and he failed not to tyrannize over his unlucky crew.

The previous night Witney and the captain had been dining ashore with some friends, and had returned to the yacht shortly before midnight rather the worse for liquor. Witney being in a bullying humour aroused the whole crew, and declared his intention of getting under weigh that very night. On being informed that it would be necessary to take in a supply of fresh meat, butter, milk, etc., which could not possibly be procured until the following morning, he postponed his departure till the opening of the shops, vowing vengeance if the yacht was not under weigh by the time he should be up. Having instructed Phillips to shape the vessel's course for Brest, he turned in. Thus it was, that at ten o'clock on this lovely April morning, " The Zouave " was bowling along towards the open channel.

The captain, whose recollection of Witney's orders of the previous night was hazy, was not a little surprised on looking out at the dead-eye to see the green water rushing past as the clipper tore through it at the rate of nine or ten knots an hour.

"I say, George, what's up? we are under weigh!" began he in a husky voice. "Under weigh; of course we are," returned Witney; "don't you remember I took 'em on the ground hop last night?"

"Ah! to be sure," said the captain, "so you did; nothing like keeping them up to the mark; my throat is awfully dry somehow, George. What do you say to a brandy and soda?"

"I had one half-an-hour ago," replied Witney, "shall I order one for you?"

The captain's answer may be guessed, and presently Filcher arrived with the drink.

Filcher having only joined the previous afternoon, the captain had not seen him before. Leach looked hard at the valet for some moments, and then burst into an immoderate fit of laughter.

" What, ' 'Zekiel,' you here ! " exclaimed he, " well, I'm bles't, if this don't lick cock fighting ! "

" At your service, cap'n ! " said that polite domestic, with a grin of satisfaction.

After the death of Mr. John Tyrrell, Filcher had, amongst other situations, filled that of messman to the ——th ; and as it was generally believed in the regiment that Leach and the messman had " squared" little matters on certain occasions, the dismissal of the one followed rapidly on the retirement of the other.

Witney was unacquainted with the particulars of the gallant captain's retirement, and knew nothing about Filcher having been messman to the ——th. He therefore learnt with extreme satisfaction that he had procured an invaluable domestic in Filcher.

" Chuck this away, 'Zekiel," said the captain, pointing to the brandy and soda, " and make us one of those cunning drinks for which you were so famous, a regular corpse-revivor, you know."

"That fellow is worth his weight in gold," continued Leach, "you are a lucky fellow, George, to come across him; makes the best pick-me-up I ever drank, a useful knave in every respect, I warrant you."

Filcher soon appeared with the cunning mixture, which was voted excellent by these parched heroes; so effectual, indeed, did the pick-me-up prove, that by mid-day (after an hour or more on deck) the captain thought he could "do" a little breakfast; so a dainty little meal was served, and with the aid of sundry provocatives and a toothful of prime cognac, the yachtsmen did fair justice to the viands.

Witney and Leach both professed to love sport; in reality one was as little a sportsman as the other. All Leach's successes had been accomplished abroad, and he had some wonderful stories on all sorts of sporting topics. If the ownership of a quantity of rifles, guns, rods, and gear of all descriptions constitute a sportsman, Witney should have been at the top of the tree; none of his implements, however, showed much wear, and if there is any cruelty in fishing or shooting, it must, in Witney's case at least, have been infinitesimal. Salmon-fishing was the idea now. " Where could they get some salmon-fishing ? " enquired Witney.

" Now look you here, George, my boy," began the captain, "if its salmon-fishing you're after, I remember when we were in Canada."

" Oh, Canada be —— ! " replied Witney, " I've heard that story three times lately; besides I want to get at it at once. There are lots of salmon nearer than Canada."

" Ask Filcher," suggested Leach.

" What the devil does Filcher know about salmon-fishing ? " continued Witney, who was growing irascible.

" My dear George," urged Leach, " you little know what a treasure you possess in my old acquaintance 'Zekiel ; he used to be regarded in the regiment as a walking encyclopædia."

" Here, Filcher ! " shouted, he as that worthy's

head was disappearing down the companion, "Is there any good salmon-fishing on the French coast?"

"Salmon-fishing, sir!" replied Filcher, "celebrated for it, sir! hardly a stream running into the sea but what's full on 'em, more especially on the coasts of Normandy and Brittany."

Leach looked triumphantly at his companion.

"I think I could show you some excellent sport, if you will take my recommendation," continued the valet. "I once travelled with a gentleman who had capital sport on the D—— river."

"I suppose you can gaff a fish then?" enquired Leach.

"And tie flies?" asked Witney.

"And splice a rod?" continued the captain.

Filcher remembered the time when all this was child's play to him, and did not doubt but that he might still be able to turn his hand to account.

Early on the following morning they anchored at Brest, where the yacht was replenished with

dairy produce, and Witney purchased some
maps of the neighbouring country showing the
different streams. Phillips retained their French
pilot, and on the following day they got under
weigh on their " coasting " expedition.

CHAPTER XII.

THE CAPTAIN'S MISHAP.

" We may say of angling as Dr. Boteler said of strawberries, ' Doubtless God could have made a better berry, but doubtless God never
did ; ' and so, if I might be judge, God never did make a more calm,
quiet, innocent recreation than fishing."

ISAAK WALTON—*The Complete Angler.*

WHEREVER there was snug anchorage . the
" Zouave " would drop her anchor, and our
enthusiasts, attended by Filcher, would set off
for the nearest river. As yet they had not
succeeded in landing a fish ; their luck seemed
to be dead out. That there were plenty of
fish in the rivers was certain, as they had seen
them almost everywhere but out of the water.
Witney, by his own account, had "moved"
three or four, and hooked one, which of course
got off. The captain vowed he had been on to

a big fish for more than an hour, when he lost him in some extraordinary and unaccountable manner.

Their plan was for Witney to fish one run and Leach another, Filcher being posted half-way between them, so as to be ready if required. This idea originated with Filcher, who laid much stress on the importance of having some one who knew how to use the gaff. As the sailor who carried the refreshments had as much idea of gaffing a salmon as riding a steeple-chase, it would manifestly have been very unfair for Filcher to have given his valuable services to one only of the fishermen.

Another great point that Filcher insisted on was to keep away from the river out of sight of the fish. Accordingly 'Zekiel and Jack (who was voted fit for nothing but carrying the provisions) used to retire some fifty paces from the river (just out of reach of the flies), lay down amongst the high bracken, out with the lunch, and amuse themselves according to the bent of their inclination.

If the weather was warm, they generally indulged in a nap, their somnolency being doubtless produced by the lulling murmuring noise of the river, and the composing influence of the liquor, of which a good supply was invariably taken. At other times they would loll about and blow their 'baccy, and laugh at the unsuccessful exertions of their energetic master and his friend.

On the third or fourth morning of the fishing expedition, the party were engaged as above described. Filcher, having refreshed himself to his heart's content, had stretched himself out for a nap, but Jack, who had no inclination to sleep that morning himself, was not much entertained by the music which proceeded from his companion as he lay, with his mouth open, on his back at full length.

"Get up, you fool," said Jack, giving the prostrate Filcher a hearty kick, "you be going to sleep; you'll be wanted directly."

"Asleep! Nonsense!" replied 'Zekiel, getting up and rubbing his eyes, and lustily denying the fact, though he had been snoring violently for the past quarter of an hour.

"Wanted!" continued he derisively, "No trees about here, are there? and not many rocks in the river. I brought 'em here 'cause they shouldn't 'itch their lines up."

"But supposing either on 'em should 'ook a fish?" suggested Jack.

"Fish!" replied Mr. Filcher with great contempt, "fish! if I a'int wanted till one of them 'ooks a salmon, I'm right. Just give that there bottle a push this way, Jack."

Mr. Filcher having had a glass of wine, changed the conversation.

"That's not bad sherry," he began, "'ardly dry enough, perhaps, but I don't quarrel with it."

"Dry enough!" exclaimed Jack, "Why, 'Zekiel, you beant half awake. How can drink be dry? If a pal means standing, he says to me, says he, let's turn in here, Jack, and have a wet; don't he?"

Filcher felt it would be hopeless to try to

explain the term to his companion, so he merely passed the bottle back in silence, with an air of superiority. Jack, curious to see this *dry-wet*, as he termed it, took a gulp, but spit it all out.

Poor Sherry that!" cried he, "I don't believe there's a drop of spirit in it."

Filcher had just composed himself for a second nap, when another lusty kick from Jack disturbed his equanimity.

"Shiver my timbers if there 'ain't something up!" Here 'Zekiel, get up—look sharp!" shouted Jack, applying his toe a second time to the carcase of the unfortunate valet, "here's the guv'ner a 'ollering and the cap'en a running—come, look sharp, I say, and bring that boat-hook of your'n along with you."

Witney had hooked a salmon. The fact of the matter was, that wearied with flogging the stream, he had sat down on a rock to rest, with his great two-handed rod over his shoulder, and the line in the running water. He was sitting with his back to the stickle watching the exer-

tions of Leach, who was industriously flogging
away about two hundred yards up stream of
him, when he was greatly surprised by a sudden
jerk and a tremendous splashing. What with
the jerk and turning round quickly to learn the
cause of the splashing, he nearly lost his balance,
and fell off the rock on which he was seated.
However, he recovered himself, and saw to his
delight the line travelling about the pool, and
the quivering of the top piece. He was sure he
had a fish, but he felt much surprised that the
fish did not use more exertion to get away ; he
thought the salmon must be a very small one,
and that it would redound more to his credit
to kill the fish unassisted than with the aid of
Filcher's gaff. With this idea he put his hand
to the winch, and was just going to wind him
in, when "whish" went the reel, as the salmon
made such a run as only a clean fish can.

If Witney thought he had but a small fish on
before, he was now quite as firmly convinced
that it was a " whopper " ; he therefore shouted
to Filcher, Leach, and Jack, with all his might.

The captain had put down his rod, and arrived about the same time as the others. The excitement was intense. "Isn't he a beauty?" said Witney, proudly, to the captain, as the fish, somewhat exhausted with his run, came slowly towards the surface, looking as yellow as a guinea.

"He seems a tidy fish," answered the captain, who to tell the truth was rather annoyed at the prospect of his companion's landing the first fish," but, "Lord bless you, when we were in Canada—"

"Come, come, old fellow," replied Witney, "let's kill the fish, and I promise to listen to the story afterwards."

It was not the fault of honest Jack that the salmon was killed. Immediately the fish became visible under the surface of the water, he threw at him the biggest pebble he could find, and pronouncing his effort—"a —— fine shot," was going to repeat the performance on the next opportunity, had he not been cautioned by Filcher against such atrocities. The effect of

Jack's " fine shot " was another splendid run on
the part of the salmon, ending with a clear jump
of three feet or more out of the water.   Had he
not been unusually firmly hooked, Witney must
have lost him.   More, however, by good luck
than good management, the tackle held, and
the threatened dissolution of partnership was
averted.   .

Witney was standing on a rock in mid-stream,
and in order to bring the fish into a place where
he could be gaffed, he had to spring from stone
to stone to gain the bank.   The captain, in his
excitement had, by stepping from one rock to
another, got as close to Witney as he could
without wetting his feet, of which he had an
infinite horror.   He was standing looking over
into the pool beneath, when Witney jumping
quickly on to an adjoining rock, slipped his foot
on some wet moss growing on the boulder, and
in his anxiety to save himself, with his unen-
cumbered hand grasped at the nearest support.
His outstretched arm came in contact with
the unfortunate captain, who was precipitated

into the pool beneath, where he and the fast expiring salmon floundered about in equal distress. Knowing that his companion could swim, and that he was in no danger, Witney thought only of securing the fish, which being, after one or two attempts, successfully landed, Filcher was despatched to the lower end of the pool to gaff the captain, who had been borne down by the current.

After some trouble Leach was dragged out, execrating fearfully, having received no injuries but a wetting and two or three prods, occasioned by the zealous Filcher's ineffectual attempts to gaff him. After a long pull at the brandy-bottle the gallant captain revived, but his unexpected immersion rendered a return home necessary. Neither Witney nor Leach were very good tempered for the rest of the day. The captain was exceedingly annoyed at having been knocked into the river, and Witney cursed the accident as having curtailed the day's sport.

CHAPTER XIII.

SOMETHING BETTER THAN SALMON.

" Hush! my dear, lie still and slumber;
 Holy angels guard thy bed ;
 Heav'nly blessings without number
 Gently falling on thy head."

WATTS—*A Cradle Hymn.*

THE young men did not remain long at any of
the different streams, but coasted along in
search of still better waters. Filcher had informed them of a magnificent salmon river
further to the southward, and, the weather
being bright and unpromising for sport, the
following day was devoted to getting to the
harbour, from which this much vaunted stream
was most accessible. On the same night,
though somewhat late, the " Zouave " dropped

her anchor amongst the boats belonging to the
fishermen of Sainte-Croix. Great was the surprise and excitement of the natives of that
quiet village on seeing the strange form of the
handsome raking craft early on the following
morning, and various were the conjectures as to
the object of her visit. For a yacht to enter
Sainte-Croix was quite an event, but such a
yacht as the "Zouave" the good folks could not
have believed walked the water.

The sportsmen were up betimes, and having
run the gauntlet of the curious inhabitants, hired
a couple of animals, and rode away towards the
river, which was a few miles distant from the
village. Annette and Christine naturally peeped
out between the blinds at the illustrious stran-
gers. The weather was still bright and hot, and
as far as sport was concerned the gentlemen
might as well have stayed at home ; but as we
before stated, our sportsmen had more zeal than
experience. Now the captain was very jealous
of Witney since he had caught the first fish,
and this feeling was not diminished by the cold

bath which he unintentionally took on that occasion. Great was his inward delight then, when, with a succession of oaths, his fellow-piscator (who had got foul of a rock) announced the smash of his rod, and his intention of giving up for the day. Now was Leach's chance! He had the river to himself, and whilst pretending to sympathize with his companion's misfortune, he chuckled within himself, and thought how industriously he would flog every likely run, buoyed up by the hope of beating his rival!

Having done ample justice to the lunch, Witney rode slowly towards Sainte-Croix, inwardly praying that the captain might not be lucky enough to catch a fish.

Returning the horse to the person from whom he had been borrowed, Witney walked towards the shore with the intention of hailing the yacht, which was lying farther off the shore than the bulk of the fishing boats. To gain the nearest point to his vessel Witney strolled past the quay, and along the rocky shore, and was searching for a convenient place for his dingy to put in, when he caught sight of a female figure seated on the rocks within a few paces of where he stood.   An agreeable contrast to the uncouth peasantry, to which the young man's eyes were fast growing accustomed, was this fair young form.   How fresh and fair she looked after the Breton and Norman peasants!   She appeared about seventeen years of age—a beautiful bud bursting as it were into the full blossom of womanhood.   Her dress was black and simple, but very different withal from the garb of the poorest classes.   There was a neatness and style about the girl which Witney could not have believed to exist in these out-of-the-way places.   Never had the native head-dress seemed becoming before.

Unconscious of his presence, the girl sat with her elbow on her knee, and her little chin resting on the palm of her hand, watching the scene, and seemingly lost in admiration of the "Zouave," which was airing some of her snowy canvass in the evening breeze.   The girl's light brown tresses played about her neck, discovering more than one shade, as the radiance of the setting sun fell upon them. Concealing himself from her view, the better to feast his eyes on the fair girl, Witney wondered within himself who she could be.

" A luscious morsel," muttered he, " what a pity for her to waste her sweetness on the desert air ! By Jove ! I'll go and speak to her."

Hardly, however, had he taken two paces forwards, when it suddenly occurred to him that the fair creature's knowledge of his language was probably as limited as his of French. His footstep, however, had aroused her from her reverie, and it was too late to draw back.

" Pardon, Mam'selle ! " began Witney, lifting his hat as he brushed close past her, under pretence of getting close to the water's edge to hail the yacht.

Christine (for it was Madame Lejeune's younger daughter) rose from the rock on which she had been sitting, and moved aside to make more room for Witney to pass. That gentleman

was sorely tempted to enter into such a conversation with the young girl as his knowledge of
the language would have permitted, but suddenly
seemed to think better of it, and placing his
whistle to his lips, he blew a shrill blast, which
was instantly heard on board the "Zouave,"
and in a few moments his boat was on its way
towards him.

The sight of this young girl had a great effect
on Witney, and he longed for the return of the
captain, that he might talk over her beauty, and
conjecture as to who she possibly could be.
That she was not a mere peasant girl he felt
assured.

Since their father's death Annette and
Christine had more than ever been cared for
by Madame Lorin; the melancholy circumstances of the fate of Henri and Pierre seemed
to bind the association between the bereaved
mother and the fatherless girls, and Annette
and Christine were educated as her own girl
Julie.

On this evening Christine having got over

her day's work had strolled out to have a peep at the beautiful yacht. Such a sight was quite novel to her; she could hardly believe such a beautiful craft could be the property of one man, and kept merely for purposes of pleasure.

About two hours after Witney had got on board the captain returned in great glee. He had got a nice salmon, and vowed that by the most cursed ill-luck he had lost another, which, of course, was twice, if not three times as heavy as the one he had killed. Leach's equanimity was perfectly restored, and his ducking quite forgotten. He was relating his exploits to his companion in the state cabin that night, when Witney, whose thoughts were evidently far away from fishing, suddenly broke in with, "Oh, curse the salmon, old man! I came across something to-day worth all the fish in the N—— river a hundred times over."

" Indeed ? " asked Leach, pretending to feel intensely interested; " what on earth was it, George ? "

" A petticoat," laconically answered Witney."

The captain's pretended interest instantly became genuine.

"Come, come, George!" said he, "I can't believe that you have seen in these out-of-the-way parts a woman who could have interested you."

"Fact!" replied Witney. "Leach! I must have that girl." The captain gave a low whistle, indicative of his surprise at Witney's susceptibility.

"I think it might be managed," continued Witney; "let me have the benefit of your advice."

"Well," said Leach, "if you are really determined to have this girl, whoever she may be, the thing must be done quietly."

"Stratagem, I suppose?" asked Witney.

"Decidedly;" returned the captain, "my advice is to tell Filcher the state of the case, and leave it to him." The valet was called into the state-cabin, and soon put in possession of the facts of the case. The omniscient Filcher seemed to know the young lady in question;

he had, he said, seen her in the village; and the three entered into a consultation which proved no good to the poor girl.

The next evening Christine was taking her walk on the shore when she was met by Mr. Filcher, who, in his best French, asked her to inform him who, in the village, could supply the yacht with milk, butter, and eggs.

As the girl turned to reply Filcher started. Perhaps he was astonished at her beauty, or at her replying to him in English. He instantly recovered his equanimity, however. Christine had guessed by his accent that he was an Englishman, and therefore had answered him in his native tongue, of which, thanks to her intimacy with Madame Lorin, she had a very fair knowledge.

Christine informed him that her mother would gladly supply the articles required, adding, that she would herself take him to her mother's house.

On arriving at Madame Lejeune's the valet purchased the articles which he professed to

want, and asked for a receipt, which was given
him, signed "Marie Lejeune." Filcher rubbed
his eyes as if doubtful whether he was awake, and
having satisfied himself on the point, pocketed
the receipt, and bade Madame good day.

The supply of dairy produce purchased by
Filcher being considerable, the good-natured
Christine volunteered to lend him a hand in
carrying them down to the quay. Filcher
praised the yacht and her fittings, and asked
Christine if she were ever on board a vessel like
the "Zouave." Christine never had been on
board a vessel of this class, and much longed
to go. Filcher assured her that this was a
capital opportunity for her, as his master and
his companion were both ashore, and would not
be back for two hours or more. The yacht's
boat was alongside the quay, and, tempted by
curiosity, and overcome by the persuasions of
Filcher, the girl stepped into the boat, and was
quickly rowed alongside.

Witney and the captain, who had been
watching the proceedings through the tele-

scope from one of the ports of the state-cabin, on seeing the approach of the boat with Christine, immediately retired to their sleeping cabins. The whole plot had been well and deeply laid. Phillips had been sent to his cabin with orders to consult the charts and lay the ship's course, as Witney intended to get under weigh that night. The two men who had been sent in the boat had been well plied with grog by Filcher after they got on board. The rest of the crew knew not whether the young lady had not come on board to take a cruise of her own free will. Whichever was the case, it could be no business of theirs.

Christine was escorted by Filcher all over the vessel. Her surprise at the luxury and convenience of everything on board knew no bounds, and the artful valet took care to interest her by explaining the use of every article. The evening was very fine, and the gentle breeze from the land scarcely ruffled the surface of the water. Having shipped her moorings (she was merely fast to the moorings of one of

the fishing-boats) the "Zouave" stole quietly
and quickly away before the fine breeze, and
so smoothly did she glide through the water,
that no one could have imagined she was under
weigh.   After a deal of persuasion Filcher
persuaded Christine to take a glass of sherry.
This done his task was easy enough, the opiate
he had put in it being sufficient to ensure un-
consciousness for the next three or four hours
at least.

The drug soon did its work, and in less than
a quarter of an hour the resistless form of the
fair girl was laid in the berth of the little cabin
in which she was destined to pass this and
many succeeding nights.   Filcher's arduous
task being over, he hastened to apprise his
master of his complete success, of which he
had ample evidence, by showing him the unfortunate Christine, as she lay in blissful ignorance of the evil that had befallen her, in the
little narrow berth.   So bewitching was the
sight, that the libertine could not resist calling
his companion to share his ecstasy.

"There!" cried Witney triumphantly, "Did I not tell you she was worth all the salmon in the world?" The captain said nothing, but his bloodshot eyes eagerly devoured the fair form and sweet innocent countenance.

The breeze freshened, the clipper tore through the water with the wind on her quarter; the shores of Normandy were fast fading in the approaching darkness, all was still and lonely. The "Zouave" was bound for the North Sea.

CHAPTER XIV.

TWO OVER-WORKED STUDENTS.

" Just at the age 'twixt boy and youth,
When thought is speech and speech is truth."
Scott—*Marmion.*

Shortly after attaining his seventeenth year,
our young friend Paul Tyrrell had been articled
to a firm of solicitors at the neighbouring seaport town of Westhampton, distant some nine
or ten miles from Beechwood. Messrs Hookham & Land had been the legal advisers of the
family for a number of years, and enjoyed a
pretty extensive practice in Westhampton and
its vicinity.

In few professions, if any, are you more
independent than in that of the law. You are
not liable to be ordered about from place to

place like unfortunate soldiers and sailors, or to be disturbed at unholy hours like doctors. You close your office at a certain hour; and if any one wants to see you after that hour, he can call again to-morrow, he knows what time the office will be open. Clients do not require half so much personal attention as patients. You can go away for a month's time (leaving your business in the hands of a competent managing man) without damaging your practice in the least. The army is all very well for young men with plenty of money, who can afford to spend £700 or £800 a year and their pay, and exchange out of a regiment ordered to any unhealthy or undesirable station; but still there must be the sense of not being one's own master. The same objection applies to the navy. In short, the legal gentleman who practises on his own account, with a sharp, trustworthy business-like managing clerk under him, and with a fair connection, has a decidedly good billet.

Paul was "reading for the law." Before

being allowed to practise for himself, a young man has to serve under articles of clerkship for five years, and (now-a-days) to pass an examination. Reading was, as may be imagined, for the first four years at least, entirely a fiction, and Paul had, like most other law-students, a very easy time of it.

In the same office as Paul was another articled clerk of about the same standing, by name Philip Rattle, a good-tempered, jovial, careless dog, who liked to enjoy his life and see others enjoy theirs.

These two were fast friends, indeed, such "chums" had they become that they lodged together, Paul having persuaded Rattle to take up his abode at the lodging-house of Mrs. Betsy Curtis, a good old creature who had nursed Paul in his infancy, and had been in his father's service for a great number of years. When Paul and his sister no longer required a nurse, and Mrs. Curtis had reached an age which prevented her doing much household work, Mr. Tyrrell had assisted her in taking a house in Westhampton, which she now let out in furnished apartments. Naturally, therefore, Paul became old Betsy's lodger, his father being glad to put him under such safe keeping, and Rattle found his friend's "digging," as he called it, so much more comfortable than his own, that he soon removed his Penates to the house of the kind old widow.

Both these young gentlemen were of a troublesome age, and the poor old lady had her work cut out to keep them in order. Frequently she would wring her hands and regret the premature decease of "Curtis—poor, dear man "—feeling how far better equal he would have been to the task.

" Mr. Paul," she would say, "was bad enough in all conscience ; but Mr. Rattle, he was a proper young limb." Many were the practical jokes which this young worthy used to play on poor old Betsy,—concealing her wig, and setting innumerable booby-traps to ensnare the poor old soul. She made every allowance, however, for the eccentricities of youth, and took these pranks in good part. Her conscience, however, could not permit her young lodgers to have a latch-key, consequently she was frequently disturbed at unholy hours of the night.

Let us see how these hard-working young students pass their evenings.

Whilst their fond mammas at home are picturing to themselves their dutiful sons plodding away at dreadfully dry books, with a wet towel round the head, and anxiously praying that their health may not suffer from over-study, Mr. Philip Rattle and Mr. Paul Tyrrell are thus employed. The former, seated in a comfortable arm-chair, with his heels resting on Mrs. Curtis's mantel-piece, calmly watches the smoke of his cigar, which for want of something better to do he blows from his mouth in rings; the latter stretched at full length on the sofa, is lazily scanning the contents of the evening paper. A short meerschaum pipe adorns his mouth. There is beer on the table, but both seem too indolent to help themselves. They

did not often trouble the office before eleven
o'clock, and their hours of attendance were by
no means regular.

Mr. Land, however, was an easy going sort of
gentleman, and made no comment on this want
of punctuality; and as the senior partner, Mr.
Hookham, never arrived before a quarter after
eleven, there was no occasion for any unseemly
hurry in the morning. And here we must, to
a certain extent, justify the proceedings of these
young gentlemen. There is a wide difference
between the salaried clerk and an articled clerk.
The time of the latter is his own, that of the
former belongs to his employer. The articled
clerk pays (or has paid for him) a large sum of
money, in consideration of which he is to be
taught the profession of an attorney-at-law, and
a solicitor of the High Court of Chancery. The
articled clerk has the run of the office, but the
gentlemen who pocket the premium do not, as
a rule, put themselves much out of the way to
instruct their pupils.

Many seem to have an idea that their craft

is to be taught by employing their articled clerks in fair copying, and therefore require them to do what a mere salaried clerk would do much better. Paul and his friend very properly objected to being made menials, and Messrs. Hookham & Land · soon found out that the services of their pupils would not enable them to economize in the matter of clerks. Both young men had served about two years of their articles, and if they took matters easy at the office, they took them, if possible, easier at home, for the dread of an impending examination was unknown in those days.

Rattle as well as Paul was passionately fond of the water, and between them they kept a small pleasure boat of about six tons. During the summer months they were cruising nearly every day, and by constant experience had really learnt to manage their little craft in a very creditable manner.

Mr. Rattle was *au fait* at most things, and was always (in his own opinion at least) making conquests of the sex. This evening he

is treating Paul to an account of some little
amourette of which he was the hero, and whilst
he is spinning his yarn let us see what has become of the " Zouave."

CHAPTER XV.

" The man that lays his hand upon a woman
Save in the way of kindness, is a wretch
Whom 'twere gross flattery to name a coward."

TOBIN—*Honeymoon.*

THE yacht's course had been shaped for the extreme north of Scotland, and being well pro-
visioned no port was touched. North, still
north, past the Orkneys, the Shetlands, and
Färoe, into the wild North Sea. Little traffic
is there here compared to that of more southern
waters. Save perhaps a few Scotch fishing
smacks, or an occasional whaler, no sail meets
the eye. A dreary expanse of water is that
between Thorshaven and the coast of Iceland.

A few hours after the coast of Normandy had

been left astern, poor Christine had recovered her senses only to find how cruelly she had been ensnared.

Young and innocent as she was, she was quite at a loss to understand why she had been thus treated. Alone, amongst some fifteen or sixteen rough men, and those men foreigners, cooped up in her little cabin, her situation would have enlisted the sympathy of any but the heartless libertines who had compassed her destruction.

No wonder that she could neither eat nor sleep. Happily her previous life had accustomed her to the motion of sea-going vessels, and she was at least free from the horrors of sea-sickness. After all what is bodily suffering to mental agony? With an aching heart, poor Christine thought of the anguish which her mysterious disappearance must be causing her dear mother and sister.

The poor young girl had been subjected to the brutal insults of Witney ; she had repulsed his overtures with becoming indignation ; no violence had as yet been offered, but she was in constant dread of what would happen next. She had now been on board five days, during which time she had scarcely left her cabin. One friend, however, had she found amongst the yacht's crew — Jem Marline—the mate. Under pretence of seeing to her comfort, the honest young fellow had introduced himself to her, and from her received a confirmation of that which he had previously suspected. Jem was not the man to stand by and see a woman outraged, and great was his delight to find that poor Christine could speak and understand his own lingo. He lost no time in telling her that Witney was a most unprincipled scoundrel— that he had carried her off with the intention of accomplishing her ruin, and had shaped the yacht's course to these unfrequented waters to avoid pursuit and possible detection. Christine could understand but little of Jem's conversation, owing to his broad county accent; but she gathered enough to learn what she had to dread, and that Jem was her friend.

" Aboard this 'ere craft," says Jem, " tisn't

'one and all,' as we say in Cornwall; the
guv'ner he's got his mates, and there's me as
has got my mates, but there's four or five new
hands along with us, and I can't hardly tell who
they'd mate with. But never you fear, miss,
Jem Marline won't see a craft in distress and
never heave her so much as a tow-line, and if
that 'ere blackguard tries to run into you, I
knows one as 'll damage his figure-head."

The greater part of this was Greek to Christine, but Jem's gesticulations spoke more strong-
ly than his words, and the girl felt assured that
he would stand by her.

And now the coast of Iceland was in sight,
and bleak and inhospitable it looked. The
snow-capped summit of Hekla was visible in the
distance, and, still far off as they were from
land, the snow appeared to lie right down to the
water's edge; but on nearing the island, however, they found that the snow in reality lay on
the tops of precipitous cliffs some 800 or 900
feet above the sea-level. A strange sight, indeed,
is the first view of the Icelandic coast. Here

and there may be seen a huge whale "blowing" a column of water to a height of thirty or forty feet. Myriads of aquatic birds are swimming in all directions. The cut-water of the "Zouave" almost strikes them as she glides through the water, which is so clear that to a great depth may be seen the divers, guillemots, and ducks diving to avoid the intruding vessel. Great splashes here and there betray the descent of the gannets, or solan geese, as they drop perpendicularly on their unsuspecting prey. Farther off may be observed a flock of these birds presenting the appearance of a snow storm, each bird appearing no larger than a flake. The noise of the various birds is deafening; here, indeed, nature reigns supreme. At intervals the yacht passes a huge inaccessible rock, glistening white as snow, so thickly is it covered with the refuse of the feathered tribe by which it is so densely populated—the home of the gannet, the cormorant, the eider-duck, the guillemot, the gull, the diver, the puffin, the razor-bill, the rock dove, the oyster-catcher, and the tern.

Safe indeed are their nests from the intrusion of man! Well may the spectator exclaim, "How wonderful are Thy works, O Lord!"

Witney evidently had not chosen these out-of-the-way waters out of mere curiosity.

The crew, however, did not appreciate the voyage they were undertaking—to be a whole week perhaps on blue water did not suit them. A general feeling of discontent sprang up, and they began to consult with one another as to the probable length of the cruise, and their destination. Jem Marline observed this, and resolved to take advantage of their disaffection. He knew that to protect this poor girl, as he had determined to do, would be an act of mutiny, that Witney would order him to be confined, and that unless he could get the bulk of the crew on his side, it would fare badly with him, and worse with Christine.

Jem therefore lost no opportunity of grumbling at the voyage, and painting Iceland as the worst spot in the known world.

"Look'ee here, mates," said he, to the crew

who were collected together in the forecastle of the yacht, taking their evening allowance of rum, "are we going to be such tarnation fools as to allow ourselves to be wintered up here in these latitudes? None of you have been in the Polar regions, or you wouldn't take matters so easy. If the guv'ner gets ashore here he's as likely to stop six weeks as one, and then, mind you, we are here for the winter, as in another month or so the ice will be down, and we shall not be able to get through it. Another thing, my lads, how comes this gal aboard of us? Is she here for any good? If there's ever a man among you he won't stand off on the other tack, after seeing a craft hoist signals of distress? Who brought her off?"

"Ned Richards and me," replied one of the men, "she came off 'long with the valet of her own accord to look over us. I never knew no other but she'd been put ashore again, 'till I found we were under weigh."

"How was that?" enquired Jem.

"Well, you see, ar'ter we brought her aboard,

Mr. Filcher he asks us down to take a drop 'long with him, and, —— me if I call to mind much afterwards ; do you, Ned ? "

" No more than you, Bill," said Ned, " I do mind though 'twas much better grog than this 'ere," continued he, tossing off the contents of his rummer.

" As I thought," said Jem ; " a plant,—a —— sneaking cowardly plant. Mates, you won't have this, will you ? "

" No, no! —— if we do ! " shouted half-a-dozen voices.

" I tell you what it is," quietly began an old man, named Purvis ; " we'll 'bout ship, and home again ! what d'ye say, lads ? "

" Ay, ay, so we will ! " assented the malcontents.

Accordingly it was that night arranged that on a signal being given on the following day by Jem, the yacht's course was to be altered, and Witney was, if necessary, to be told that he was no longer considered captain of his own vessel.

On the morning of the following day Christine was visited by Witney, who in vain renewed the solicitations which she had hitherto successfully repulsed. Exasperated by her firmness and unflinching courage, Witney would have attempted force. Remembering the promise made her, Christine screamed, and a moment after the cabin door was burst open with a crash, and Jem Marline, armed with a boat's stretcher, appeared on the scene.

"Come out of that, you lubberly swab!" shouted he, seizing the astonished Witney by the coat-collar, and hurling him to the other end of the cabin.

" Come, slip your moorings, this 'ere bean't no anchorage ground for you ! "

Witney was speechless from mingled fright and astonishment, and apprehensive of further rough usage from Jem retired precipitately to the state cabin, where he found the captain, and in a hurried and excited manner narrated to him what had occurred.

"My dear George," began Leach, "I must

blame you. It's your doing—your own fault entirely—you never take 'em on the ground hop; I remember when I was in Canada—"

"Here, Filcher," shouted Witney, "go seize the —— mutinous dog, and put him in irons."

But somehow or other Filcher did not seem to relish the chance of an encounter with the sturdy young tar who stood up defiantly before him, so he rushed off for assistance, shouting lustily to several of the yacht's crew. Two or three sailors responded, and were ordered by the infuriated Witney to bind Jem and put him in irons.

Great was the astonishment of the owner of the yacht, when, instead of his orders being promptly executed, one of the hands exclaimed, "Seize him yourself, you blackguard, we don't do no dirty work for you!" "Ay! ay!! seize him yourself, you cowardly lubber!" echoed the others, "we've had enough of this 'ere job and sailed far north enough to please you, now damn you, you shall sail south to please us."

Witney saw that the men were determined,

and that discretion would be the better part of valour, so he betook himself to the captain's cabin to discuss the awkward situation in which they found themselves. Meanwhile Jem had comforted Christine, and made her understand that no harm should come to her. He took possession of the cabin next hers, that he might in case of need be near to protect her. He might have spared himself the trouble of changing berths, however, as Witney was far too frightened to meditate any further violence. All was disorder and confusion on board the "Zouave." The skipper of the yacht was at his wit's end—he knew not what to do. On learning the diabolical trick that had been played upon Christine he was very indignant, and could scarcely but applaud the decision at which the crew had arrived. On the other hand he was captain of the craft, and his duty was to preserve order and discipline on board, and obey his master's orders. He resolved therefore to take no active part on one side or the other, and quietly represented to Witney that the vessel was evidently at the mercy of the crew, that he was sorry that Witney's conduct should have caused the mutiny, that if he continued the command he would be deprived of it as soon as ever anything displeasing to the mutineers occurred, and, in short, that he preferred resigning his berth.

Jem Marline was unanimously elected "cap'en;" orders were given to 'bout-ship, and the clipper was soon tearing away in the direction from which she had come. Jem Marline being a smart young fellow knew enough of navigation to lay the yacht's course, and having told off the watches, he proceeded to take possession of the keys, that the crew might not get at the spirit-lockers, which they are apt to do on such occasions.

Witney, Leach, and Filcher spent a most dreary time of it; they fared as the common men, and scarcely dared show their faces on deck; whilst Christine was treated like a princess, and walked the quarter-deck as if she were mistress of the vessel. Jem Marline had quite determined on seeing Christine safely out of her trouble, and his intention was to quit the " Zouave " on arriving in England, and to take the poor girl to his mother's house in Cornwall. In due course they made Aberdeen, where they touched to get a few necessaries, and then sailed for the Isle of Wight, their starting-point.

When within a few miles of the island, Jem took Christine off in one of the yacht's boats, so as to get a clear start of Witney, and they were soon on their journey towards Marline's home. Christine's heart was light again, for she knew she was in honest hands. On reaching Jem's home Madame Lejeune was at once written to, and great was the joy at Sainte-Croix when tidings of the lost sheep arrived. For some time past the fisherman's widow had entertained thoughts of removing to England, where she thought there might be more scope for her daughters, who would of course have to work for their bread. Little inducement was there left for the poor woman to remain at Sainte-Croix, the scene of her greatest troubles.

On hearing of Christine's safety and whereabouts, she therefore determined on selling the
little house and her belongings, going to England, to reclaim Christine, and taking up her
abode there.   In less than two months the Lejeunes found themselves at Penruthan, a small
fishing village on the Cornish coast, the home
and birth-place of the brave Jem, who had so
gallantly saved Christine from the ills which
threatened her.   One of the Sainte-Croix boats
had put them across, so the cost of removal was
not great.   Finding Mrs. Marline an honest
good-natured old person, and the village cheap
and convenient, Madame Lejeune decided on
(for a time at least) making Penruthan her
home ; and a cottage within a stone's throw
of Jem's was obtained for her through his influence with the landlord.

Very pleasant the young girls found Penruthan, and quite contented would they have
been to remain as they were.   But the widow
was now living on the proceeds of the sale of
her house and fishing-boats.   She therefore

saw the necessity of her girls obtaining employment.

With a view to getting pupils in music, or French, Annette was despatched with a little ready money to Westhampton, Christine being kept at home as company to her mother, and Jem Marline, whose kindness and bravery had made a wonderful impression on them both.

CHAPTER XVI.

SECRETS OF THE LAW.

" Variety's the very spice of life,
That gives it all its flavour."
COWPER—*The Time-piece.*

MR PHIL RATTLE on this point, at least, agreed
with the poet Cowper. We left him entertaining Paul with an account of his last conquest;
we should have said " then last," for we find
him now (but six months after) engaged in a
similar way; but on this occasion the heroine
was a far superior creature to her of whom he
had, but a short time since, been so proud.
This was " positively the last." By this time
Paul quite understood the peculiarities of his
vivacious friend—quicksilver was tranquil compared to Phil Rattle, who, however, considered

himself the most unchangeable of admirers. The then present admiration was always the one *par excellence*—the out-and-outer—until he saw some one he admired more, and wondered how he could have been imposed on by such mediocre charms as those of the one who had just lost his regard.

Paul listened with as little attention as usual. He was the reverse of his friend ; that is to say, he was not what is now-a-days termed "gushing ;" he generally kept his own counsel, but to-night he longed to unburden his mind, and relate to his friend an adventure which had that day befallen him.

What an indescribable relief it is to impart to a friend the subject which engrosses all our thoughts !

Is it that we feel the matter too much for our individual brain, or why ?

How often do we disclose our secrets, and feel relieved by so doing, all the while suspecting (and but too often rightly) that we are making fools of ourselves !

Undoubtedly the pleasure of a secret consists in imparting it to another. How one itches to tell a third party anything " between you and me, you know." Twenty times had Paul been on the point of narrating his adventure to his friend—twenty times had he postponed it, not knowing how to begin, and doubtful whether after all it would not be wiser to keep his own counsel.

At last out it came, and Paul wondered what could have prevented his telling it to Rattle half-an-hour ago.

" Your conquests are all very well, Phil," began our hero, " as far as they go ; but hitherto you do not appear to me to have got beyond a work-girl, or, at most, a little milliner. I wonder what you would have thought of the fair creature I met this afternoon—none of your vulgarians without an 'h' about them—but a regular little lady speaking French better than English, so stylish, and such a handsome face ! When I say 'little,' you know, I don't mean she is short, on the contrary, she is a very fine

grown girl ; I only used the epithet ' little ' as
a term of endearment ; but you shall see her,
Phil, you shall see her, old boy, and if she
doesn't take the shine out of all your nymphs,
my name's not Paul Tyrrell ! "

Phil looked half-annoyed, half-astounded.
It was his principal delusion that the sex found
him totally irresistible ; he could not help feeling jealous of Paul's luck, and calculating what
a tremendous impression he would have made
had he been in his friend's place. He, however,
thought it advisable to " pooh, pooh " the young
lady, and caution Paul against French refugees,
and so forth.

Seeing Phil's humour, Paul thought it unad-
visable to say more about his adventure that
evening, and so the subject dropped.

CHAPTER XVII.

" If to her share some female errors fall
Look on her face, and you'll forget them all."
POPE—*The Rape of the Lock.*

THE following afternoon at three o'clock, our
hero found himself by the sea-side, about a mile
from the town of Westhampton. He wandered
to and fro with a listless air, and kept looking
at his watch, and round the corner of the road-
way, as if he expected some one. Nor was he
doomed to disappointment, for in a few minutes
a tall comely looking girl tripped up to him and
bade him good afternoon in the most self-pos-
sessed manner. Having returned the salutation, Paul pulled the girl's arm through his
own, and led her by a by-path to the beach.

"I was so afraid you would disappoint me," began Paul—"that you would not come."

"But," returned the girl, who seemed much of an age with the young student, "Did I not promise?"

"Certainly, you promised," replied Paul; "but young ladies, I know, from experience, do not always keep promises of that kind."

"To me a promise is a promise," said the young girl, slowly and thoughtfully, as if she too had had experience of broken vows.

"And my word is my bond," returned Paul, "as I thought yesterday, you are a girl after my own heart; by the way, what am I to call you,—you told me your name was——"

"Annette," added the girl; "but do not call me so, call me anything short—anything, but that."

"Well then, what do you say to Nannie?" asked the young man; "that is a pretty name."

"Yes, yes, that will do capitally," laughed his companion.

They walked on for some time in silence,

until coming to a large flat rock on the beach, Paul suggested that they should sit down, to which proposition Annette made no objection.

" M'sieur," asked the girl, after seeming to reflect for some time, "you are ' triste,' you think very much, is it that I displease you? Tell me, what wrong have I done ? "

The fact of the matter was, Paul found himself in a very uncomfortable position. Only the previous afternoon this young girl had modestly and politely enquired her way -to a certain street, and Paul seeing how handsome she was, had, under pretence that his own road lay in that direction, accompanied her to the place she wished to reach. Naturally vivacious, their conversation became rapid and confidential, and before they parted, Paul had laid Annette under a requisition to meet him the following afternoon, which she had very imprudently, perhaps, consented to do. Thus it came about that these young people were sitting together on the same flat stone on the beach.

" And how long have you been in Westhampton, Mam'selle ? " asked Paul.

" Only a few days," returned the girl ; I know
no one here, it is so lonely ; but what would
you ?—one must live, and I am arrived here
quite alone to endeavour to get some pupils."

" Pupils !" echoed the young man, " so you
teach, then ? and what may you teach ? "

" As yet," replied Annette, " I have been unsuccessful in my attempt to get pupils, so have
taught nothing ; but I know enough of your
language to enable me. to teach mine, and I
can play and sing. When we met yesterday I
was on my way to the house of a lady, who I
expect will engage me to teach her girls music ;
I hope indeed she will, for it is most expensive
to remain here earning nothing, and I am sure
my mother cannot afford to give me more
money."

" So you have a mother ? " said Paul, enquiringly ; " how then is it that she is not with
you ? "

" A town like this is too dear for one of us,"

returned the girl sorrowfully, "how then could three of us afford to live here?"

"But I suppose," argued our hero, "your father can do something for your mother and yourself?"

An expression of grief came over Annette's countenance, as she told Paul that she had lost her father some two years ago.

The kind-hearted young fellow saw that he had been too hasty in his conjectures, and apologized for his thoughtlessness.

This last unhappy shot of his prevented his cross-examining his companion further, and for some time he maintained silence, wondering who the third person in the family could be.

Annette saw his curiosity, and came to the rescue.

"You would admire my sister," said she, "she is very beautiful—so fair, not like me. Ah! but Christine! elle est jolie comme un cœur!"

"And you are not, I suppose," interrupted Paul. "I wonder whether you really think yourself less good-looking than your sister! All I know is, if she is handsomer than you, she must be a clipper!"

"A what?" asked Annette, "qu'est ce que vous voulez dere?—a cleep-are! I know not at all such a word."

"Ah, naturally," replied Paul, "you cannot be expected to understand a word which I had no business to use. I merely meant that your sister must be uncommonly handsome."

"And so she is, M'sieur," rejoined the elder sister, proudly.

"I can quite believe it, if she bears any family likeness to you," said the young man, looking tenderly and admiringly on the exquisite features of the young girl sitting beside him.

Paul was, as Annette had remarked, extremely thoughtful and silent. To tell the truth he felt heartily ashamed of himself. To gratify his vanity he had forced his society upon this handsome girl, in perfect ignorance of her station, birth, and antecedents.

We must not disguise facts ; Paul was a young

man, and wild as a colt, frisky and full of life. A love of adventure, of a pretty face, and the chance of an intrigue had prompted him to cultivate the girl's acquaintance. He had, like other young men, done the same thing a dozen times before with various success.

Like most young men he was silly, and thought it the thing to be sceptical about the virtue of women, and on his first meeting with Annette, we more than half fear that any display of virtuous indignation on her part would not have been appreciated by him as it should. This afternoon, however, he had not been in the company of the girl a quarter of an hour, before he felt convinced that he was talking to as virtuous a creature as God had ever made, and could not but hate himself for having ever entertained doubts of her purity. What would the girl think of him could she know the thoughts he had harboured?

Poor Annette! she had not thought at all! She had been but a few weeks in England, and till her arrival in Cornwall had lived all her life

at the small fishing village on the coast of
Normandy.

In all innocence had she accepted Paul's
proposal to escort her to her destination on the
previous evening, and to take her for a walk
the following day; and our hero must be for-
given if to a certain extent he had misunder-
stood her, for unsophisticated innocence was a
rare article in Westhampton. But now, as
Annette, in her light prattling conversation,
from time to time betrayed her ignorance and
guilelessness, the young student felt that instead of leading this fair young thing into
temptation, it should have been his part to
shelter her from the dangers which must beset
a beautiful young girl living alone in a gay
town in a foreign country.

Paul was no advocate for wanton cruelty,
and would not for worlds intentionally place a
stumbling-block in an innocent woman's path.

Here was a girl worthy in every respect, so
far as he could judge, of his lasting love and
esteem, and the reckless young fellow gazed

admiringly on her and thought how he should have cursed himself if he had injured such a woman as the one who sat by him.

Such were Paul's thoughts. What were those of Annette? We remember her sitting before the fire in her old home at Sainte-Croix; she was thinking then, and had thought on from that time until the death of Lorin; but after his fate and that of her father, what was left for poor Annette?

For months she gave way to that bitter grief which seems to expend itself in its intensity, but at last the welcome change came. Grief cannot last for ever; time is the great healer: and now, two years after the wreck, Annette was again at times the light-hearted, merry, careless girl she was before the reader knew her.

The temporary loss of Christine, and anxiety for her safety, had of course damped her spirits; but now Christine had been brought back in safety, she was full of life and health, and the bustle and excitement of Westhampton, the largest town she had as yet been in, elevated her wonderfully.

Although Annette's usual manner was, as we have said, blithe and gay, there were times at which recollection of past events pained her terribly; and at such times she would be downcast, moody, and silent. This, however, was one of the girl's bright days—a day on which to meet her one would never believe that she had ever known trouble.

To-day she felt no care for past, present, or future; to-morrow all three periods might cause her the greatest concern—so buoyant was her nature.

Her companion remained silent and thoughtful, an unusual thing for the light-hearted young man. What his thoughts were we have endeavoured to describe. He seemed lost in admiration at the beautiful girl beside him. As a rule he had no lack of impudence, and on the slightest provocation would make nothing of putting his arm round a girl's waist and kissing her. But with Annette he was com-

pletely non-plussed. He neither knew what
to do or say : in all his life he had never felt
so much disposed for love-passages and so
utterly incapable of commencing the siege.
The fair creature seemed unintentionally to
hold him as it were at arm's length.

It was the month of November, and the
days were shortening rapidly. The approach
of darkness reminded the young couple of the
hour ; and, with a mingled feeling of relief and
regret, Paul conducted his companion towards
the town, the gas-lights of which could already
be seen shining dimly through the foggy,
clammy atmosphere. Paul's courage revived
with the increasing darkness, and we fear that
as our hero sauntered along with Annette's arm
linked in his, he was guilty of many of those
little hand-squeezings which speak so much
more loudly than words. Who can doubt the
existence of animal magnetism ? Surely not
those who have experienced the thrill occasioned by the caresses of love, whether by the
impassioned kiss, or the gentle pressure of the

hand. How intensely gratifying to woman's nature it is to feel that she is the one loved by a man above all the rest of her sex! Few women indeed can fail to appreciate such a compliment as this, even though she doubt the value of the love proffered her—fewer still can fail to reciprocate the love of a man whom they believe fully entitled to their's.

Thus it was with Annette. Brought up as she had been, she was to a great extent unconscious of her beauty. She had not been spoilt, as too many pretty girls are, by constantly having their beauty pointed out to them. Hence our hero's attentions to her were the more appreciated.

Paul saw her home to the street in which she lodged, and an appointment was made to meet on the following day.

So things went on, and in three weeks time the young people were unquestionably in love with each other. Annette had been fortunate enough to procure some half-a-dozen pupils, and was earning enough to pay her way, and occasionally make a small remittance to her mother.

Phil Rattle had been introduced to her, and found her society so agreeable that he was fast forgetting his mortification at his friend's luck. Mr. Rattle soon announced to Betsy Curtis that a young cousin of his was staying in the town, and would one evening honour Paul and himself with her company at tea. The good old lady was at first rather sceptical about the relationship ; but when Annette arrived, she was so delighted with " the young person from France," as she persisted in calling her, that her doubts soon vanished. The fact was, the good old lady could not manage the French name Lejeune, and after two or three attempts at the pronunciation, in which she treated Annette's patronymic most barbarously, gave up in disgust.

Mrs. Curtis could not refrain from expressing her astonishment that "the young person " should be about so much by herself, and was inclined to be curious about her relations ; but

Rattle was always equal to the occasion. He would begin some extraordinary romance, and gradually entice the old landlady away from the subject, the result being that poor old Betsy knew no more at the end of his yarn than before.

Annette's visits became very frequent, and very pleasant were the long evenings spent by the three young people. Annette would play the old worn-out piano, and sometimes sing with Paul, whilst Phil would persist in accompanying the vocalists with his banjo.

Although Annette was very fond of Phil, it must not be imagined that her regard for him was of the same nature as that she entertained for Paul. Nothing was done without Paul's advice and sanction, and day by day the ties of their mutual love were drawn more closely.

CHAPTER XVIII.

ANNETTE'S CONFESSION.

" Let me not to the marriage of true minds
Admit impediments. Love is not love
Which alters when it alteration finds."
SHAKSPEARE—*Sonnet CXVI.*

PAUL and Annette had frequent opportunities
for tête-a-tête. They generally walked out of
an afternoon if the weather were at all fine :
indeed, each began to feel the society of the
other indispensable. Rattle, like a good-
hearted fellow, seeing how attached his friend
was to the girl, would often find engagements
which he feared would deprive him of the
pleasure of their society. In short, he took
himself out of the way, " that the young people
(Phil was about six months older than Paul)
might do a quiet spoon."

On one of these occasions Paul and Annette were sitting by the fire, when somehow or other the conversation turned upon their youthful reminiscences. Paul had been narrating some little incident which occurred to him as a boy, when he perceived that Annette's eyes were full of tears. This evening she had allowed her recollections to overcome her. To Paul, who had never before witnessed one of the girl's melancholy fits, her grief was inexplicable. In an instant his arms were thrown round her neck, and in the most anxious tone he begged to be informed what ailed her.

"Oh! nothing, nothing," was Annette's womanly reply; but the young man saw plainly that he had unintentionally brought to the girl's memory some painful event which she shrunk from telling him. In vain he attempted to soothe her, and bid her dry her tears. At last, when she had become a little calmer, Paul again demanded the cause of her emotion.

"Oh, Paul! dear Paul!" exclaimed she,

"do not ask me! Spare me! Do not let anything interrupt our happiness — and yet I should have no secrets from you. But what if I should forfeit your love? The thought is too much for me."

The young man was thoroughly amazed. What secret could Annette have the knowledge of which could possibly cause his love for her to decrease?

"For Heaven's sake, Nannie," cried he, "put an end to this mystery! I am sure you are making a great fuss about some very little occurrence. Come, tell me all about it, like a dear old girl!" And Paul seated himself in the arm-chair, drew the girl gently on to his lap, and rested her head on his breast.

Annette's fine earnest eyes looked up into her lover's face enquiringly, as if to ask how the intelligence would be received. Finding nothing to discourage her in Paul's expression, she began slowly and seriously.

"Listen, Paul. No living creature but myself knows the secret which I shall now reveal to you. A secret should exist between two persons only."

She paused.

During all this time Annette was seated in Paul's lap, her head resting on his breast. Could the young fellow do less than hug the pretty girl whose form was encircled within his arms? Would any hero be tolerated who could refrain from snatching kisses under such circumstances?

It was not the first time that the young couple had found themselves in this dangerous position, but never before to-night had Annette's manner been so impassioned and unrestrained. Paul was surprised; for, affectionate as the girl had always shown herself, there had always hitherto been a certain retiring modesty about her which indeed had, as the reader will remember at their first rendez-vous, tended to repulse our hero's advances. This evening, however, overcome with recollections of past events and present happiness, her self-control seemed to have deserted her, and she returned

Paul's warm caresses in a manner which left no doubt in his mind as to her sincerity.

"Oh! Paul, dear," continued she, "I feel so happy; but yet I feel I have no business here. I know now what a miserable wretch I am: would to Heaven that I had known three years ago what I know now! I dread to tell you, dearest—you will never love me any more."

"Why, Nannie," returned the young man in a gay tone, "I shall think you have committed some horrible murder or robbed a church, if you go on condemning yourself so. Come, come; open confession is good for the soul; your crime is venial enough, I'll warrant!"

After some hesitation the poor girl told Paul her melancholy story — how she had loved Lorin, not wisely, but too well—how young and innocent she was at the time—how her sister had been carried off in the yacht, and rescued from dishonour by the bravery of Marline— how her mother had sold her house and effects, and crossed the channel with her to reclaim Christine —and lastly, how she came to be resident in Westhampton, teaching French and music.

Paul had listened attentively to the poor girl's narrative, and, though he felt a slight pang of disappointment at learning his beloved was not what he had hitherto believed her, he was so convinced that she, when a trusting and innocent girl, had been heartlessly betrayed, that his sympathy for her was aroused, and he felt that it would be hard indeed if the misfortune which had befallen her could in any wise lessen his love for her; and his indignation at Lorin's conduct knew no bounds.

"And where," cried he, jumping up, and nearly upsetting Annette, "is this scoundrel— this Lorin?"

"Hush, Paul!" whispered the girl gently; "Henri would have made me his wife: he told me, when he went abroad, that on his return home he would ask his mother to consent to our union ——"

"Which he knew very well his mother would refuse!" broke in Paul, angrily. "I tell you,

Annette, the man who would betray a young and innocent girl would not hesitate to break his word.   Where is the villain? "

" Beyond the reach of your reproaches," replied Annette, gravely.   " He is dead—was drowned within sight of my old home on the same night as my dear father ——"

" A judgment on him, say 1! " interrupted the young man, hastily.

" On my father? " asked the girl.

" No, no—on Lorin," returned Paul.   " Was your father then drowned at the same time ?"

" Alas ! yes," replied Annette with a sigh. " What a fearful night that was !   Little did I think, when I went out in the boat with father, who was on board that unlucky ship."

" Do you mean to say you went to sea with your father in such a night?   What good could you have been in a gale of wind? "

Annette laughed at Paul's scepticism as to her knowledge of boat management, and told him the horrors of that night as we have already described them.

Our hero was delighted with the girl's skill and bravery, and secretly determined that she should teach Phil Rattle (who fancied himself a perfect sailor) how to sail the little six-ton craft they owned between them. How disgusted poor Phil would be!

Few evenings passed of which Annette did not spend the greater part in Paul's rooms, and she had become, as Phil Rattle observed, " quite an institution."

" Oh! Paul darling ! " exclaimed Annette one evening, as she threw her arms affectionately around him, " how I wish we could be always together—the days seem so long without you ! "

" Really, Nannie," answered Paul, " I don't see why you shouldn't. Mrs. Curtis has a nice room to let. What do you say to changing your lodgings ? I wonder we never thought of it before."

" Oh! if I could but do that ! " continued the girl, clapping her hands with delight. " Will you let me, Paul ? But what do you think Mr. Rattle will say? I could make your tea and breakfast, couldn't I?"

"Oh, Phil be hanged!" returned Paul, "besides he'll be pleased enough, I'll warrant."

Finally it was arranged that Mrs. Curtis should be spoken to on the subject.

Poor old Betsy's one idea was to let her lodgings, and though she would perhaps have preferred an English lady to "the young person from France," the opportunity was too good to be lost. The following week therefore found Mademoiselle Lejeune domiciled at Mrs. Curtis's lodgings. The "young person" was supposed to take her meals in her own room, but the gentlemen found her so useful at their table, that it was not long before she messed with them. This plan saved Betsy Curtis a deal of trouble, and as the old soul did nearly all the work herself, having only the assistance of the unlucky maid-of-all-work (such an institution in lodgings), it suited her well.

The good old lady, of course, looked upon

"the young person from France" as Mr. Rattle's cousin.

Mrs. Curtis had little to do with Annette's room, as that young lady made her own bed, and looked after her own affairs. One morning, however, Betsy had occasion to go to Annette's chamber at an unholy hour of the night. Two or three gentle raps did the old lady give at the door, but no response. After a time, thinking Annette was in a sound sleep, she gently pushed the door open and walked in. To her amazement and horror "the young person from France" was not there,—evidently no one had slept in her bed that night.

Mrs. Curtis rubbed her eyes and looked round the room, and in the cupboard, and under the bed, as if she thought her lodger might be in any of those places, and wished to give her the benefit of the doubt. The old lady's thoughts were almost unsupportable.

That "young limb," Mr. Rattle, was at the bottom of this, she would be bound! Betsy waited at least half-an-hour in Annette's room, and finding she did not return, determined on visiting the room again the following night.

Poor Betsy ! her worst suspicions were then confirmed, and she vowed dreadful things against that " young hemp of a Rattle, and that there deceitful young person from France."

CHAPTER XIX.

MRS. CURTIS RECONCILED.

But Faith, fanatic Faith, once wedded fast
To some dear falsehood, hugs it to the last.

MOORE—*Veiled Prophet of Khorassan.*

THE following morning Mr. Rattle was "inter-viewed" by Mrs. Curtis, when some smart dialogue took place. Phil was perfectly ignorant of the cause of his landlady's indignation, and the old lady was exasperated beyond measure, because she thought Rattle's ignorance was assumed. Betsy opened fire with a broad-side. "You young wiper," cried she, thrusting open the door of the room in which Phil was taking his breakfast, "you wicked young hemp! To think that you, a friend of Mr. Paul's (which you was recommended by him to me) should bring me to this."

" Bring you to what ? " enquired Phil with an astonished air, "you are not brought to the work-house, are you ? "

" Worse than that, much worse than that," whined the old woman, putting the corner of her apron to her eye.

" Pawn-shop ? " suggested Rattle, " nonsense, Betsy, you are not come to that surely ! Oh, I say, —— it, I'd sooner have paid you something on account, you know ! Why didn't you ask me for it, instead of coming here bullying me like this ? I daresay I could have borrowed a flimsy.

" And do you think, Mr. Rattle, sir, that because I am poor I am to be bribed by an early settlement of what is justly due to me ? "

" Bribed ! " roared Phil, " who thought of bribing you? Why in the name of goodness should I bribe you ? "

" Come, come, Mr. Rattle," said Betsy, " 'tis no use your carrying on and making believe— I caught her ——"

" Caught *her!* caught who? " asked Phil, going towards Betsy, and sniffing enquiringly, as if uncertain as to whether she had been imbibing something with her tea that morning.

" Don't smell of it, anyhow! " said he to himself. " I hope the old girl isn't going off her nut ! "

Mrs. Curtis was now sobbing violently, and talking very incoherently about the respectability of her house, her late lamented husband, and her impending ruin.

" Tell us who you caught ? " continued Phil, " that maid of yours has been prigging, I suppose ? "

" That wicked young person from France," sobbed Mrs. Curtis, " now don't look so innocent, if you please ! "

" What, prigging? Oh, I say, come, you know, this won't do ; my cousin ain't a thief! "

" Which thieving is nothing to it," retorted

his landlady, " but she shan't stop in the house a day longer—not an hour ! "

" Pray collect yourself, Mrs. Curtis," said Rattle, in a more serious tone, "and tell me with what crime you charge Annette, for I give you my honour I don't understand a word of what you are saying."

It was such an unusual occurrence for Phil to speak seriously, that Mrs. Curtis could not fail to remark his sincere tone, and began to wonder whether she had not put the saddle on the wrong horse. She therefore deemed it prudent to say no more to Rattle on the subject, but to go straight to Annette for an explanation. She was on the point of abruptly withdrawing, when Phil prevented her, saying, " Well, Mrs. Curtis, you have blackguarded me pretty considerably, I wish to know of what you accuse me ? "

" All in good time, sir, all in good time," returned the old woman, evasively ; and gaining the door she left the room, leaving Phil quite bewildered.

Annette was sitting in her own room mending socks when Betsy entered.

The girl looked up from her work, and kindly bade her " Good morning."

"Don't 'good morning' me, you wicked deceitful hussey!" returned Mrs. Curtis, confronting her, " I've found out your nasty Frenchified ways, and out of this house you go this instant!"

Poor Annette did not understand all the speech, but the landlady's tone and gesticulations convinced her that she was the subject of her abuse.

" How have I offended Madame?" asked she, simply.

"Drat her imperence!" shrieked Betsy, "well, I never! and she sitting there as if butter wouldn't melt in her mouth. Now then, Miss Parley-voo, where was you last night! Not in your own room, anyhow?"

" In my own room ?" repeated Annette, " no, certainly not; I have not slept there for weeks past. You see Paul's is larger and more comfortable."

"And you dare to tell me this to my face?" said her landlady; "why, you don't seem the least ashamed of yourself."

"Why should I?" returned the girl, "I love Paul. I know that many people think there is no marriage without the usual ceremony at church, but Paul is my husband for all that, and I am his wife."

Mrs. Curtis began to wonder whether the young people had been united at the Registrar Office, and looked furtively at Annette's hand, to see if there were a wedding-ring on her finger.

"Wife or no wife," said Betsy, "you h'an't got no ring; and these 'ere Frenchified ways won't do for me. May the Lord forgive you both! Poor Mr. Paul, too, whom I nursed as a child, to think that ever he should have been sedooced and led away like this. What will his dear papa and mamma say—and to happen in my house, too! Oh dear, oh dear! O you wicked forward young hussey!"

Having obtained a full confession from Annette, Betsy bounced off to attack our hero.

Towards him, however, she seemed to evince more pity than anger, and after dilating for some time on the care and attention she had bestowed on his youthful training, and on what a bitter disappointment it was to her to see him grown up into such a wicked young man, gave vent to tears.

"I need not tell you, Mr. Paul," said Mrs. Curtis, "that the young person cannot stay another night in my house."

"Certainly not, against your wish, Betsy," said Paul. "You of course understand, however, that if Annette leaves your house I leave with her. Be good enough to ask her after she has packed her own things to pack mine, when we will at once go in search of other lodgings."

Betsy winced; she did not like the idea of losing two lodgers, and one of them such a lodger as Paul, for whom Mr. Tyrrell paid on the most liberal scale.

Paul noticed the effect of his speech, and hastened to follow up his advantage.

" You see, Betsy," continued he, " puting
aside the question whether or not this familiarity
between Mademoiselle Lejeune and myself is
improper (a question which I do not think it
necessary to discuss) your declining to let us
your apartments any longer will not prevent
our continuing to live together. There are
other lodgings to be had in Westhampton,
though it is but just to you to say, that I doubt
whether we shall succeed in finding such clean
and comfortable quarters elsewhere."

In the course of the day Paul related to Rattle what had occurred, and told him that as he
was quite determined not to give up Annette,
he feared they would be no longer able to
occupy the same lodgings as Phil.

" Oh, nonsense !" said that young gentleman,
" don't listen to what that old fool says, stop on
as you are ; it will be all right again in a few
days. I'll go at once and tell the old girl that
after the manner in which she has treated my
cousin it will be impossible for me to remain
here any longer—that will frighten her ; I guess

she can't afford to lose all her lodgers, besides, I will point out to her that when your father hears you have changed your diggings, he will find out that the girl was permitted by Betsy to visit here. I know she can't afford to offend your father. Leave it to me, Paul, leave it to me; I worked the oracle for you to get Annette here, and I'll work it to keep her here."

With a most serious face, and the air of one who has been deeply injured, Phil sought out Betsy, and gave her notice that he should quit if Paul and Annette were turned out, and even had the impudence to ask for an apology for the insult offered to his cousin.

The poor old landlady was non-plussed. She had not anticipated losing either Paul or Rattle; it was a time of the year at which there was little or no demand for lodging accommodation at Westhampton, and Mrs. Curtis felt that it would probably be a long time before she could succeed in letting any of her apartments; as for letting all, she knew it was out

of the question. On the other hand, how could
she countenance such "goings-on" as she was
pleased to term them ? To be at once deprived of the income she derived from her
lodgers, was ruin to the poor old lady. She
had no other source of revenue but them, and
even had her credit been sufficiently good,
she could not afford to run into debt. Clearly
the matter required most serious consideration.
In the meantime Annette was busy packing
her own trunks as well as Paul's, and Phil
made a great show of preparation for a speedy
departure. Towards the evening Mr. Rattle
received a second visit from Mrs. Curtis, for
which he was not altogether unprepared. His
demeanour and conversation were so diplomatic,
that at the conclusion of the interview, it was
arranged that Paul and Annette should be re-
quested to stay that night in the house, as Mrs.
Curtis didn't wish "to part in anger." At the
same time, Phil doubted much whether the
harshly-treated individuals would remain an
hour longer than necessary under Mrs. Curtis's

roof.   He, however, would persuade them if
possible to do so.

Mrs. Curtis's lodgers did not leave that day,
or the following day, or the day after that; and
after the lapse of a week or so, the landlady
became satisfied in her own mind that the
young couple had been lawfully joined in the
bonds of holy matrimony, an idea which Phil
nursed with his wonted *savoir-faire*, by hinting
that it was a profound secret, and begging her
not to divulge it.   Poor old soul ! the wish that
it might be so begot the thought that it was so,
and the infant thought gained strength with
time, and thrived on Rattle's blarney.   The
Court of Chancery looks on that which ought
to be done as done, and if Betsy was not a
Chancery advocate, she was at least an equitable
old woman.   She begged Annette to wear a
plain gold ring, and when this request was
acceded to, her mind was more at ease.

Madame Lejeune was delighted to hear of
her daughter's success as an instructress, and
threatened two or three times coming up to

Westhampton to pay her a visit. Annette, however, dissuaded her from doing this, representing to her that her pupils' holidays would soon afford her the opportunity of running down to Penruthan to see her and Christine.

END OF VOL. I.

MISCELLANEOUS WORKS.

LIVERPOOL:

ROWLAND A. ELLIOTT, 42 CANNING PLACE.

MISCELLANEOUS WORKS.

---o---

STRAYED, BUT NOT LOST. A Novel. By
MERLIN. Two Vols., 8vo, cloth extra,   21s.

THREE LITTLE FRIENDS. By A. BOWER.
One Vol., 8vo, cloth,   10s. 6d.

ESSAYS ON EVERY-DAY LIFE, for Old and
Young. By 'NON PAS.' One Vol., 8vo, cloth extra,
10s. 6d.

> Ch. 1. Introductory remarks—Value of sympathy in our
> homes—'Say a kind word when you can.'
> 2. Love and friendship.
> 3. Happy and miserable people.
> 4. Pet animals.
> 5. Sorrows of others as compared with our own.
> 6. Misrepresentations, prejudices, and backbiting.
> 7. Servants.
> 8. Children.
> 9. Masters.
> 10. Religion at home.

OUT IN THE COLD. An Annual. Large 8vo, 6d.

CONTENTS.

Seasonable Pictures, No. 1	To Love
Up in a Garret	Seasonable Pictures, No. 2
Song of Father Christmas	My Aunt's Present
The Hansom Ghost	Ned Willoughby's Christmas
The Sonnet Wave	A Parting
The Haunted House	'Stand off them Points'
'A Merry Christmas'	The Mystery of Kindelay Hall

THE UNION MAGAZINE. Published on the
1st of each month,   6d.

LIVERPOOL TOWN-CRIER ALBUM.

4to, cloth extra, 3s.

Contains well-executed Portraits of the following well-known Persons.

Rt. Hon. R. A. Cross, M.P.,
Home Secretary.
John Laird, M.P. (The late).
Charles Turner, M.P. (The late).
Rev. T. Major Lester.
Rev. Father Nugent.
Rev. H. Stowell Brown.
A. B. Walker.
William Inman.
George Melly.
C. B. Greaves Banning.
T. S. Raffles.
Major Greig, C.B.
Joseph Rayner.
G. F. Lyster.

G. F. Deacon.
Henry Hime.
Miss Blanche Cole.
Miss Selene Dolaro.
Miss Pattie Laverne
Miss Jenny Willmore.
Miss Lizzie Willmore.
Mrs Edward Saker.
Edward Saker.
J. L. Hall.
G. W. Anson.
Henry Irving.
J. K. Emmet.
Joseph Eldred.
Sam. Hague.

STRAY LEAVES, QUARTERLY. A Magazine
of Reviews, Essays, Poems, and complete Stories. 1s.

STRAY LEAVES. A Holiday Magazine of
General Literature. 6d.

MR ELLIOTT has pleasure in informing the Trade and the Public that having succeeded to the business of Mr A. Wainwright, he is prepared to supply many of the following Books issued by the Town and Country Publishing Company, Limited.

~~~~~~~~~~~~~~~~~

FICTION.

————♦————

Charles Lysaght. A Novel Devoid of Novelty.
By P. M. BERTON. Two Vols., 8vo, cloth,   21s.

An honest attempt to portray character and to depict scenes of actual life as they have fallen under the author's own observation. The hero and his father are both well delineated, and the struggles of the former in his effort to gain a living by his own exertions, are described in a painfully vivid manner, but without any undue colouring.—*Daily News.* •

We beg to commend the novel in general. Two or three of the minor portraits are unique. No circulating library should be without it.—*Illustrated Review.*

It is written in an easy, pleasant style.—*Bookseller.*

There are some scenes and sentiments of considerable merit.—*Tablet.*

Natural gifts do not seem wanting, and there is a power displayed both of perception and characterisation.—*Sunday Times.*

In *Charles Lysaght* we have a novel which is thoroughly enjoyable from the first page of Vol. I. to the last of Vol. II. . . . . A novel so well conceived and executed has not been offered to the public for a very long time.—*Court Express.*

The writer possesses his share of quiet humour.—*Midland Counties Herald.*

There are some sketches of character and many descriptive passages by no means wanting in skill.—*Era.*

Notwithstanding the title, there is a 'novelty' about this novel which will be found very refreshing.—*Alfreton Journal.*

By Hook or by Crook. A Novel. By O. D. Y.
One Vol., 8vo, cloth,   10s. 6d.

Agnes Ingold's Money. By E. C. S. Two Vols.,
crown 8vo,   21s.

If Either—Which? A Novel. By T. P. W. Two
Vols., crown 8vo,   21s.

'Nameless.' A Novel. By F. A. N. One Vol., 10s. 6d.

The story hurries the reader on with untiring interest, and describes the relations of the characters with great skill.—*Sunday Times*.

'The Cloudy Porch.' A Novel. By SARAH G. LANGLEY. One Vol., demy 8vo, 10s. 6d.

'The cloudy porch, oft opening on the sun.'—*Tennyson*.

Wrecked Early in Life. A Story. By HEATHER One Vol., demy 8vo, 10s. 6d.

This is a story with local attractions, the scene being partly laid in this neighbourhood, and the matrimonial finale being enacted in that most popular Welsh watering-place, Llandudno. The heroine is one of the most loveable and noble women, who has to leave the house of a vulgar and tyrannical step-father because she will not marry a husband of his own choosing. This step-father was 'one of the most extensive coal-mine proprietors in West Lanca-shire.' He purchased an estate, with mansion, park, and pleasure-ground, within a couple of hours' drive of Liverpool, and here it was, except when at school, that the heroine spent her later child-years.—*Liverpool Courier*.

A clever but ambitious attempt at a novel of real life.—*Morning Advertiser*.

There are many clever people to be met with in these pages.—*Tablet*.

Wrecked Early in Life is unobjectionable as regards style, and is free from vulgarity.—*Hour*.

Come of Her Vow. By MEADOWS S. THORP. One Vol., 10s. 6d.

Perdita, and other Stories. By HELENE A. CASSAVETTI. One Vol., 8vo, 10s. 6d.

MISCELLANEOUS.

—o—

Scenes on Pacific Shores. With a Trip Across South America. By HENRY E. CROASDAILE (Retired Lieu-tenant R.N.) One Vol., demy 8vo, cloth, with Frontis-piece, 7s. 6d.

Scenes on Pacific Shores is an agreeable book. The best part of it, to our mind, is the latter moiety, describing a journey across the South American Continent—from Valparaiso to Buenos Ayres. But it is all readable—*Standard*.

Some pleasant glimpses—and unpleasant ones also—of the Panama route open the volume, and we journey with the author to San Francisco, a very fair description of which city and California generally is given.—*Era*.

We can speak very favourably of *Scenes on Pacific Shores*. As the experiences and thoughts of a naval officer serving on the Pacific Station, they are fresh, amusing, and sailor-like.—*Tablet*.

Mr Percy Slipscombe's Visit to the Isle of

Wight; a Series of Caricature Sketches of a Recent Six Days' Trip. By GRANTHAM JAY,   1s.

Will repay perusal.—*Figaro.*

Entirely a work of humour.—*Globe.*

The Slipscombes are a very interesting family, and we commend them to the attention and consideration of our readers.—*Hornet.*

Mr Jay evidently came here with the full intention of amusing others and being amused himself: his sketches bristle with puns, and are brimful of pungent humour. The book must be read to be appreciated.—*Isle of Wight Chronicle.*

Slipscombe is a character. He is not a Pickwick, a Dick Swiveller, a Chuzzlewit, or a Micawber; yet he seems to have a little of all these in his composition. There is a good deal of rattle in Mr Jay's narrative; and the writer not only tells his story, but tells it well. A capital book to put into a pocket or bag, if, like Mr Slipscombe, you are going on a trip to the Isle of Wight, or anywhere else.—*Bristol Times and Mirror.*

Essay on the Germs of Scepticism. By Mrs

LOUIS LE BAILLY,   1s.

How to Make a Fortune in India, with

perfect safety, in Six Years. By J. TULLOCK NASH,   6d.

On the Divorce and Marriage Laws. A

Pamphlet. By VIRGINIUS,   3d.

Wild Flowers. The Leicester Magazine. Edited by

A. J. LOSEBY (ALEXANDER PEBBLE). 64 pages, 8vo, 6d.

Summer Evenings. A Midsummer Annual. Edited

by W. F. BALFOUR,   6d.

POETRY.

—o—

A Collection of Original Poems and Songs.
By JAMES FINLOCH.   One Vol., demy 8vo, cloth,   5s.

The verse is facile and flowing, and the simpler poems on Scottish subjects contain pretty stanzas, naturally written. Here is an example:

"Down Finloch shaw the birdies woo," &c.

Here the very faults are not offensive, and the way in which the music of the verse breaks and ripples away at the end supplies a most happy instance of the genial and pathetic quality latent in a rich, broad Scotch accent.—*Illustrated Review.*

Mr Finloch possesses an enviable faculty of expressing himself in poetical terms, and his volume is in every way a creditable production.—*Bookseller.*

Tama and Zulu. By ALEXANDER PEEBLE.   Crown 8vo, cloth,   2s. 6d.

A pen which can manifestly exercise itself with much skill, force, and pathos in tender or humorous subjects. Nothing, indeed, can be finer, truer, or more exquisite than many of the touches scattered through the miscellaneous pieces with which this little volume concludes, and we can safely commend them all to the perusal of the most fastidious even of our fair readers. 'I loved her at first sight' is a gem.—*Bell's Weekly Messenger.*

Second Canto of "The Recollections of a Pebble;" with Introduction and Opening Stanzas to the First Canto. By ALEXANDER PEEBLE, Author of *Tama and Zulu.* Boards, toned paper.   1s. 6d.

Lyric Leaflets. Cloth 8vo, bevelled boards. 3s. 6d.

Gushes and Grumbles. By FREDK. LANGBRIDGE, Author of *Kitty Crump*, &c.   1s.

If the verses of Frederick Langbridge have not quite the finished polish of the poems of Frederick Locker, they are wittier and more amusing, reminding us of Carverley of Albert Smith in style and the smoothness with which they lend themselves to a carolling song. Many of the poems, indeed, are evidently written to be sung in the drawing-room. We heartily commend this little book to our readers, feeling assured they will be pleased with its brightness and ability; and we trust that we shall have further "Gushes" (and no "Grumbles") from a poet so sensible, clear-headed, and mellifluous.--*Figaro.*